For my best wishes

at Purdue Col

Cordially

Pepe Castro

Hammond, August 31, 2011

AND WHAT HAVE YOU DONE?

And What Have You Done?

* * *

A Novel by
José Castro Urioste

Translated by
Enrica J. Ardemagni

Latin American Literary Review Press
Pittsburgh, Pennsylvania

Acknowledgements:

This project was supported by the Pennsylvania Council on the
Arts, a state agency, through its regional arts funding partnership,
Pennsylvania Partners in the Arts (PPA). State government funding
comes through an annual appropriation by Pennsylvania's General
Assembly. PPA is administered in Allegheny County by Greater
Pittsburgh Arts Council.

This project is also supported by Indiana University Purdue University
Indianapolis.

Library of Congress Cataloging-in-Publication Data

Castro Urioste, José, 1961-
[Y tú qué has hecho? English]
And what have you done?: a novel / by José Castro Urioste; translated by
Enrica J. Ardemagni.
    p. cm.
ISBN 978-1-891270-25-3 (pbk.: alk. paper)
1. Boys--Peru--Fiction. 2. Voyages and travels--Fiction.
3. Maturation (Psychology)--Fiction. 4. Peru--Fiction.
I. Ardemagni, Enrica J. II. Title.
PQ8498.13.A78Y313 2009
863--dc28

                                                                    2009009626

*My deepest appreciation goes to José Castro Urioste
for his continuous help, support and patience,
and for letting me give voice to his voice.*

*I thank Juan Carlos Temprano, the king of mentors
who made me believe in my abilities,
and my best friend Michael R. Solomon
for keeping it real.*

*For the sunshine of my life,
my son Giancarlo Echarry.*

E.J.A.

It seems to me that we have walked farther than we have been walking.

- Juan Rulfo

TABLE OF CONTENTS

FIRST TAKES
(IN BLACK AND WHITE, OF COURSE)

✳ ✳ ✳

When was that *when* and that fortunate morning when I told myself, I confess that I, too, have lived, and it is clearly time that I put all of the past down in writing, because memory remains, yes it remains, but writing about the past is like taking a picture of life. Then I asked myself, okay, now where shall I begin, and I waffled back and forth, wondering if I should start from the main door of this history or if I should step through a half-open window. I was in that dilemma (and to be honest, I still am), until I said to myself again, don't complicate things, start from the very beginning. And there, of course, is when I remembered my mother and her smile, like a white cloud traversing a sunny sky. I don't remember the day that she brought me into this world—that would be the very beginning—, because it suffices to say that I don't remember it although I've heard thereabouts that on that afternoon my father had eaten *picante de mondongo*, spicy tripe, for lunch, accompanied by a hefty amount of red wine brought from the Velasquez farm itself, and from there he went to the Hipolito Unanue Hospital and he told my mother that she shouldn't worry, and that she shouldn't worry because babies are always born at night and it was barely twoish in the afternoon and he was going to swing by the stadium because the Alianza Lima team had come here to Tacna to play a soccer game with us, or rather, with Bolo, because Go Bolo! Come on Tacna! I must have heard my father. It couldn't be otherwise: I must have heard him and ever since that afternoon I began to contradict him my whole life because as soon as he finished saying, Go Bolo! Come on Tacna!, my mother said, call the doctor, and, kerplunk!, I came into this world, and my father, of course, didn't know whether he should say my son, damn, my son, or Go Bolo! Come on Tacna!

But this is not the very beginning that I remember, but rather that morning when my mother with her cloud-like smile that traverses a sunny sky told me that it was already time for me to go to school. I had already been by there two or three weeks before that with my friend Daniel, Mrs. Amanda's son, who would later become famous and known as the Dog, so well known and famous as the Dog that when he left and got married in Venezuela and when his wife was expecting a child, Mrs. Amanda said she was going to Caracas because her daughter-in-law was about to give birth and she wanted to be there to welcome the puppy. But back then he was just my friend Daniel and he didn't bark or anything and we were both there at the school to take an exam that we didn't know was an entrance exam to get into the parochial Jesuit school that was run by a priest, of course, who came from Gringoland, but not necessarily so, and they said that before he became something of a priest he had been in World War II launching bombs at Hitler and all of his gang. And then a teacher asked me questions and I answered accurately with that ballsy attitude that one only has when he's five or six years old, while my father displayed a giant screen-size grin and upon each one of my correct answers he seemed to say, that's my son, damn it, that's my son, until suddenly, of course, the teacher asks me if I know what a dozen is, and with that same ballsy attitude, I tell her, a dozen?, a dozen is a case of beer. And my father smacks his head because at that instant he can't slap me, and the teacher shows me a smile exactly like the girl in the television commercial for Arequipa beer, and sure enough, she tells me, welcome to the school. My father left leaping and jumping with joy, because that's my son, and since we had run out of Velasquez wine at home he went out to buy a case, exactly a dozen, and he didn't go to work because that's my son.

That's what the situation was when eight o'clock arrived that morning when my mother, with her cloud-like smile that traverses the sky, told me to hurry up and finish my breakfast to go to my first day of school. I finished off what was left in

my glass of milk in one big gulp and my *marraqueta* bread
sandwich of mountain cheese disappeared in two big bites. Because that was the traditional Tacnean breakfast just like the
poet Fredy Gambetta had written about in his verses, and just
like Jorge Basadre had confessed to my friend Lucho Vasquez,
waiter and head waiter for more than thirty years at a tourist
hotel, on one winter morning at that very same hotel cafeteria:
that milk and bread (*marraquetas*, that is) like those from your
native land didn't exist elsewhere, not even in one's dreams.
And my mother left me at that school which was so dang far
from town, out close to Para, where you can just about see the
airport. There were about thirty or forty of us kids there and I
recognized my friend Daniel, Mrs. Amanda's son who was still
neither famous nor known as the Dog, and there the two of us
got inside a concealed trench away from any kid that we had
not seen in the main square, nor on the beach, nor at Lucho Pit-
taluga's birthday party where everyone was so excited about
the balloons, a two-layer cake, and the purple-colored *chicha*
juice that dripped on their shirts which *Ace* detergent and "*Ña
Pancha, señora*" (as the TV ads said) were made for. Occasionally Daniel would say something to me, something oddly
profound because Daniel had been like that even as a snotty-
nosed kid, as deep as the last mile out of two hundred miles
and I don't understand how the hell he didn't end up being a
philosopher, but anyway, now he is a civil engineer and that has
given him his deepness because he makes immeasurable holes
over which he constructs his houses, hotels and all those places
where one eats, sleeps and screws peacefully without knowing
absolutely anything about its deepness. At times I paid attention to him, other times I stared at the sunny sky searching for
a cloud that might pass by. And all this happened right there
in the main courtyard of the school where the thirty or forty of
us kids who had passed the exam stood and who at that instant
didn't know what we were waiting for, if it was the lady who
would be our teacher, or the priest from Gringoland who had
pummeled Hitler himself fearlessly. That's how it was, with

an unbearable sun that made sweat run down our cheeks and soaked our shirts, when suddenly a shirt that was even sweatier than mine bumped against me and it wasn't Daniel's but rather a shirt from one of those other thirty or forty children. Then the sweaty shirt looked at me and smiled, and I gave him such a damn look of anger, even angrier than my father's when Bolo is losing four to nothing. And I looked at the sunny sky out of the corner of my eye and since I didn't see any white cloud crossing: Bam! I smacked the sweaty kid's head just because he wasn't watching where he was walking and because he was running into all of us, or rather, into me. And he told me what's wrong with you, and I looked at the sky with a dumbshit face thinking let them come and get me because it wasn't me. And this kid's attention strayed, and since I don't see any white clouds passing by, and Bam! I whack his head again just because he was sweaty, ugly, and because I get madder than my father when Bolo loses by four to nothing. Then a dark-skinned kid jumped out: It was him, the dark-skinned kid said, and of course, given such evidence and so much smacking the sweaty boy slapped me in the middle of my right cheek that left it hotter that a fritter just pulled out of boiling oil. I won't take it, I won't take it, and the dark-skinned kid yelled heating up the fight. At this point and with that cheek I was madder than my father when Bolo is losing eight to nothing, and with two of his own goals to boot, and suddenly I don't see any clouds in the sky and Bam! a smack in the head, and I won't take it, I won't take it, says the dark-skinned kid, and, Bam! my other cheek starts burning, and another whack in the head and alternate blows on each cheek, and I won't take it, I won't take it. And thus, between the head whacking and the slapping and the dark-skinned kid adding fuel to the fire, although easy yet difficult to believe with no more than that, a friendship was born that would be an understatement if I say lasted for a lifetime, because it is and continues to be a friendship that goes beyond all history.

That's the very beginning that I remember. Then month

after month passed by in which Mañuco (that was the kid's name with the sweaty shirt) and I didn't scuffle, nor did Juan Carlos (that was the dark-skinned kid's name) egg us on. Quite the opposite, we sought each other out to play kid's soccer on the same team against the others in the classroom and shortly thereafter Rudy joined us, better known as the Tank, because of his stature and the size of his pot belly. And on the dirt pitch soccer fields we were transformed into Chumpitaz, Cubillas, Perico Leon, and all the other famous players on the National Peruvian soccer team, and we would return home covered in dirt, and for that of course, *Ace* and *Ña Pancha, señora*.

Back then Miss Maruja loved us all equally and at some time all of us must have fostered Oedipus-like dreams about her. Always sweet-natured, always ours, always Maruja, always Maru, always you for those boys who look at you morning and afternoon settled in their desks and maybe day-dreaming about you without even knowing what they are dreaming about. What deception, what pain, when I ran into her twenty or thirty years later, I had known for some time what an erection was and she was becoming aware of the beginning of her aging. Miss Pat was a pretty-faced gringa with an elephant-sized body and cheerfulness larger than an elephant. Obviously she taught us English and she came to Peru with that thing known as the Peace Corps, a *Corpus Magnanimous* in her case, and she had fallen in love with this country first, and then with this small southern city in this country located smack dab in the middle of the desert. And so with a little bit of luck Miss Pat hoped to find a *Peruvian boyfriend*, a Tacnean *even better*, and to have a *Peruvian family* and learn how to cook the *picante de mondongo* that she liked so much. But there wasn't even a smattering of hope for Miss Pat because she coincided with a coup d'état and the Revolutionary Army appeared and in the name of the country nationalized the country from one end to the other, telling the Peace Corps *bye-bye*, they declared English an imperialist language regardless of who spoke it and instated the indigenous Quechua as the official language, forgetting that in former times

it had been the language of the Empire. Then Miss Pat packed
her bags holding back her tears from time to time, sometimes
not being able to restrain herself, and she went back to Gringoland without a *Peruvian boyfriend*, nor a *Peruvian family*, and
without even finishing her *English as a Second Language* class.
Of course, we never learned the imperialist language nor was
there anyone who bothered to come teach even hello and good
morning in Quechua to us, and thus we became openly and
honestly, a fanatically monolingual generation.

But neither Miss Pat nor my dreams about Miss Maru, always dear Maruja, were the source of my love at that time,
although back then I didn't even imagine that soon, very soon, I
would meet her, that I would meet you. It was five or six months
after the first day of classes when my friend Mañuco Morales
told Juan Carlos and me that weekend was his birthday, the
bastard was going to be six years old, or the little bastard as we
would say back then, and he wanted to invite us to his house
because his parents were planning a party for him with a lot
of cake, purple *chicha* drink made from corn with nothing left
over, bowls full of *palomitas* that Miss Pat called popcorn, and
a clown that came from the last circus that had been to Tacna.

So we went there and Daniel with all of his philosophi-
cal deepness that was never exposed went, and Mono, which
means Monkey, Castrejon who truly was a Monkey because he
climbed every tree that he saw until he almost broke his neck,
and his mother, Miss Maru or whoever, ran out to take him to
Hipolito Unanue Hospital to put a cast on his broken arm one
more time. We all arrived together and at the same time because
Mrs. Amanda said that she could pick us up at our houses and
leave us at the Morales' house and vice versa. Mañuco opened
the door with a whopper chicken and mayonnaise sandwich
and a piece of chicken with mayonnaise bulging from in between his mouth and cheek, and the Monkey in front of him
and running towards the back yard and to his delight he found
a peach tree that was at its peak and he took off climbing until
he reached the top, while Daniel in all of his deepness hugged

Mañuco wishing him a Happy Birthday so profoundly that the piece of chicken sandwich with mayonnaise stuck in his cheek popped out, and Juan Carlos and I ran to the sandwich table like lightening and it seemed as though our mothers had us in Easter fasting because we surrounded the chicken sandwiches, and look at these ham and cheese sandwiches and macaroons made by Mrs. Guillermina. And Mrs. Amanda, nervous as heck of course, with these kids who aren't her kids, but after all, that's how kids are.

I remember that during that afternoon we enjoyed ourselves as if we had gone to a picnic in the sky. Mañuco blew out his six candles with one blow, Juan Carlos sang parts of the words to a Tango that his father who was better known as Half Tango taught him, because he never knew an entire song, and his son would become known as Quarter Tango because he never learned more than half of a song that his father taught him. After all, the older folks celebrated this Peruvian Gardel, the Argentine king of the Tango, who we didn't even understand given half a chance. Then we played a game of kid's soccer in the back yard among the four of us (the Monkey was still climbing around in the tree) against Mañuco's cousins. And once again Chumpitaz, Cubillas and Perico Leon and all the other players of the National soccer team appeared, and all the roses, geraniums, and cresses disappeared and a huge goal by Cachito Ramirez turned a flowerpot into pieces of shit that no one noticed so go for it, go for it, and we all continued with a goal here and another there until suddenly a Tarzan yell was heard coming from the sky towards the ground that turned out to be Monkey Castrejon in full cry and landing in the middle of the soccer field. Mrs. Amanda extremely nervous and running to the soccer field where all the kids are who aren't her kids, but that's how kids are, and Mañuco's mother in a similar state but even more nervous because jeez, Amanda, this kid could have killed himself! and the two women left taking the Monkey for his nth cast and we stopped our game in honor of our fallen friend and who had experienced a bad rap on a branch which must have happened to Tarzan himself once in a while when he missed connecting one little swinging rope with another like when he was flying in the movies and on television.

That was when I got a tremendous urge to pee and I left Cubillas, Perico Leon and Cachito Ramirez. I went to the bathroom quietly and concentrated on my friend Monkey Castrejon, hoping to God that nothing has happened to him although nothing ever happens to him, because if cats have nine lives this Monkey must have more than a dozen. With that dilemma in mind I opened, entered, and closed the bathroom door when I saw a girl as large and as small as me was already in there, telling me hi, my name is Adriana, like my mommy, and my grandmother who were also named Adriana, and I live here close, very close by, two houses down that way and that's all, one pink house and one sky blue, the sky blue house is mine, have you seen it?

And I, well, speechless, more speechless than in my dreams about Miss Maru, Maruja, always dear Maruja, and Adriana asking me and you, what's your name, and I was sppeeeecccchhhlllleessss. What's wrong with you, did someone eat out your tongue? because my mommy says that children who talk and ask a lot of questions have their tongues eaten out at night, so let's see yours, do you have a tongue or did someone eat it? And I speechless and dumber than shit, stuck my tongue out as far as it would go. Yes, you have a tongue, she said, and I think that it is bigger than mine, let's see if it's bigger. Then she came close to me with the frickin' guts that only five or six year old girls have, and even though no one might believe me, she placed a finger horizontally on my tongue, and then another, and then another, and I stood there speechless as hell, dumbshit and speechless as hell and feeling a sensation that before that no one had ever told me existed, not my father, not my mother, not Miss Maru, who was so good and who loved us all equally, not Miss Pat who had come from a far-away country and who knew other things that no one else knew, not the priest Headmaster who had lived and survived an entire war, tickling Hitler himself on the stomach. So I continued, without understanding

what was going on but it was going on, while she touched my
tongue eternally with each one of her fingers. Three and a half,
she told me, yeah, your tongue measures three and a half fingers, and she pulled back her hand and I just stood there, open-
mouthed and with a hard on although I still didn't know that
expression. My tongue is smaller, it's only three fingers, but ...
then how come you don't talk?

I was saved by the bell, because at that age one not only
doesn't know how to handle an erection, he doesn't know what
the hell is happening either, just that he's got a hard on period, and within that order or disorder of things one can have
less, but even less of an explanation for one's silence caused by
an erection in the bathroom. The bell rang again, that is, Mrs.
Amanda was yelling my name throughout the house because
she had already returned with Monkey Castrejon with a cast
on his right arm and well, it was already time to take all those
kids home who aren't her kids, but that's how kids are. And she
opened the bathroom door like someone who turns off a movie
in the middle of its showing, and turns on the lights, and she
yanked me, let's go. I got back my speech and told Adriana,
Ciao, and she gestured goodbye by moving those little fingers
that had just measured my tongue and that had brought about
my first memorable erection.

Maybe by that age I already knew something, because at
that age there's shit you know without knowledge of its cause,
and at six years of age which is how old I was back then there
was only one thing I wanted: to run into Adriana again and this
time, at least this time, say something more to her that ciao.
Then I began to ask my parents' permission to visit my friend
Mañuco Morales, and then I would tell Mañuco for us to go
play in front of his house, or better a little further down, two
more houses down, Mañuco, here, here is good, right in front
of the sky blue house. And my friend Mañuco Morales always
beat me in all our games because I was standing there, looking
and looking at that sky blue house. I saw her walk by the living
room window two times, but those two times were so fleeting,

so quick, that there wasn't even time for her to realize that I was on the other side of the yard of her house. Afterwards I never saw her again. One afternoon I returned but there were no longer curtains in the windows, nor the cream-colored car that was always parked there, nor any semblance of people walking around inside the house. They had gone forever and only many years later I found out that after the military coup that dethroned the last Viceroy of Peru, that is, Belaunde, the same coup that left Miss Pat without a *Peruvian boyfriend*, that very same coup made Adriana's father and the entire family go into hiding away from Tacna because he had been working in Belaunde's viceroyalty. And all of that made me feel extremely far from her, and that distance increased my desire to find her although I didn't have a clue about where she could be, and upon finding her, of course, I would say more to her than just ciao, I would tell her, hello, my name is Ernesto, my friends call me Tito.

As An Accomplice, The Drizzle

✳ ✳ ✳

And elementary school flew by for us. It passed by almost like playing, and really life has passed us by playing, with some making more goals than Cachito Ramirez, others like Chumpitaz on defense, and like Zegarra the Chinese boy, so dumb the poor kid, called Miss Goalie, because he understood Miss Maru's explanation of noun gender the exact opposite of what it is, and that morning when we went out to recess after Spanish class, in front of the dirt pitch field where we played kid's soccer, the Chinese kid Zegarra stood firm on his legs and one hand and he, very macho of course shouting that no goal would pass through here because I am Miss Goalie. Everyone was agreeing and egging him on, although it was never discovered that the Chinese kid Zegarra (from that moment on and forever known as Miss Goalie) would turn out gay or that he would swing both ways, it was just that he understood everything backwards.

Elementary school flew by, it just went by, and in all those years I never again heard where Adriana with her three-finger tongue had gone. Peru was damned expropriated and Tacna had military flanks on all four sides and the militia displayed their tanks and machine guns in parades during patriotic festivals, and people were impressed because the only thing missing was for them to show a half-bred version of the atomic bomb, and even the same priest Headmaster from the school who had whipped out his ding-dong at Hitler, stood there with his mouth wide open at such a display of weapons and surely, more than surely, he was saying in his heart: Our Father who art in Heaven, please don't let there be war on Earth.

Thus elementary school flew by, it just passed us by, and Miss Maru, always dear Maru, told us that would be the last year that we would be together because she didn't teach in high school but nevertheless she would continue loving us all the same. Miss Goalie almost let out a few tears, although since he was so macho, or feminine as he would say, he held them back, and the Monkey remembered the twenty thousand times Miss Maru had taken him to the Hipolito Unanue Hospital to get a new cast.

She stood there, in the middle of the class, saying these six years had flown by, and elementary school had gone by, it had just passed by, but before going on to high school we had to take an exam over everything we had studied and anyone who didn't pass, well, would have to look for another private school. Another school? and everyone made a big Gulp! another school? if we were friends for life and we didn't want to separate our lives and Gulp! everything for a frickin' exam and more Gulp!, and Rudy the Tank took three extra Gulps! because that year he had discovered secretly, very secretly, what it was to jack off and in between stroking and stroking he had not written one line in his notebooks and he thought that Mama Ocllo was part of the theory of wholes. So everyone had to study, Miss Maru said, but that time, that time only, no one loved her because it seemed that she didn't love each of us equally. We forgot about being Cachito Ramirez and Chumpitaz and the rest of the Peruvian National soccer team, and we got down to studying like never before, more because of our camaraderie than anything else, more to continue that friendship than anything else. But Rudy the Tank not only sat down to study and to learn that Mama Ocllo was tied to the history of Peru rather than the theory of wholes, he also cut back on his jacking off because his older brother told him that masturbation affected one's memory and a bunch of other shit that he couldn't remember, and he also begged Señor de Locumba, a miracle worker capable of all kinds of miracles, pretty please Señor de Locumba, I beg you and double beg you to help me pass this exam because I don't want to go to another school, Señor de Locumba, and if you help me pass I promise you, for my mother's sake I promise you that I will walk from Tacna to your church that is more than 60 miles of pure desert, and after that trek I am going to walk kneeling through the entire church up to your altar and I will leave you an offering, what offering do you want, Señor de Locumba?, I will leave whatever offering you want, but pretty please, help me pass that exam.

We all passed, even Miss Goalie which was already asking too much because for the first and only time in his life he understood that the world could be straight and not backwards. Then Rudy carried two water canteens that his brother had and he left his house on a set trail: to cross the desert until he arrived at Señor de Locumba's altar. And there the Tank struck out, in the heat of the day with his canteens under his arm, and the Tank went on for about half a mile from Tacna, drinking a little water, damn, I already drank all the water, when suddenly, Wham, the dust in the desert rose up in protest against the Tank who had fainted belly-up. Rudy the Tank remained in that position for who knows how long until a truck sent by Señor de Locumba passed by, after all, the intention is what counts, that carried him to the entrance of the hospital where he found Monkey Castrejon getting his twenty-fifth cast.

Then we entered into the first year of high school and we met Professor Grover, just plain Grover not to stand on ceremony, because he was pure Tacnean, yeah, more Tacnean than *picante de mondongo* with its meat jerky and cow's hoof and its *marraqueta* bread on the side, because that is one spicy meal and healthy, man, healthy with its dry wine. That was Grover, although no one knew why he was called Grover, and on the first day of class he launched a hell of a speech that no one understood, not even Daniel in all of his deepness, but all of us had the feeling that he was going to rip us apart in high school and at that moment we thought about and missed our Miss Maru, always dear Maru.

Grover didn't miss a detail: after a few weeks of class, Juan Carlos, or Quarter Tango, showed up with some magazines of chicks in bikinis, chicks in skimpy tangas, completely naked chicks. Then Rudy the Tank felt exceptionally accompanied in this life because jacking off became an established institution with its rules and competitions and on your mark, get ready, Go!, and its winners, five in a row for chubby Lucho (Rudy the Tank extremely angry because he had never done more than four), with a long ejaculation squirt that measured one foot eight inches.

That was the year that Monkey Castrejon gave up his tree climbing forever: he became terribly afraid that one day he might break both arms. That was the year that Juan Ortega, better known as Ortega son, arrived at the school straight from Lima, who saw an immeasurable quantity of bikini-clad chicks, tanga-clad chicks, and naked chicks—including some pictures of Raquel Welch in a *Playboy* that Quarter Tango stole from his old man,—but he never participated in the masturbation competitions, and he was always embarrassed by any uncontrollable erection. That was Ortega son, with his straight-legged pants that came up almost to his chest, his short greased-down hair combed like his father demanded, who was a Commandant or a Coronal who had transferred to Tacna, because in Tacna, no one knew him, so something big was afoot.

Then this Prime Minister General Morales Bermudez arrived on August 28 for the town festivals where there is always a parade of schools and the military, and the young girls fight with each other to carry a flag through the street going from one end to the other, and at night, of course at night, there is dancing and twenty thousand songs accompanied by fireworks and a widespread mob of drunks and concentrated in Arms Square itself. General Morales Bermudez, representing his president General Velasco, came to this bash and on the night of the bash he said, Long live the Revolution! Long live General Velasco!, and even Ortega son himself with his pants up to the middle of his chest heard it on television. People say that on that night Morales was walking around talking with Ortega father and that he went to bed as a Velasco, and on the next day he got up saying, I myself am Velasco, and shitting on General Velasco who with one command from Tacna was taken out of the Governor's Palace. And the dictator was fucked, puppet dictator, Ortega father thought, shaking Morales' hand and telling him everything had gone as planned, my General, because Tacna had the largest military base in the country and now the whole country was under control, my General. That's what Ortega father said, and surely he was thinking about one more military person and who knows, no one ever knows, in a future cabinet position.

A few years went by quickly and during those years, one day, one morning in the middle of recess at 11:30, Quarter Tango said he had an invitation for a coming-out party at Gaby Castillo's house, better known as the Little Beach Lizard, because every summer she spent all her time sunbathing and overly sunbathing on rocks at the beach. That weekend we all went to the Little Beach Lizard's house, and from that weekend on, for any party anyone had, we all went as a gang and well plastered to whatever party was going on, because before going we would buy some rum with Coca Cola, and to your health, pal, because this two fingers of rum is boss, and we would down our rum right there, in the middle of Bolognesi Boulevard, leaning on the benches like a lot of other adolescent groups, and peeing from time to time on a palm tree of choice.

And at the end of those few years, one day, one morning, I believe it was during lunch break, Mañuco divulged that the family that had been his neighbors when he was a child had returned to Tacna, Adriana's family, because Velasco was no longer in power and her old man didn't have anyone to be afraid of and it seems as though he was starting a transport business here. I, just like many years ago, remained speechless. Then Daniel, already baptized and re-baptized as the Dog, said he thought he had seen her, he had seen Adriana, he had seen you, last Sunday in the main square, walking with her father and mother, but he wasn't sure, because time passes, man, and you know, the last time I saw her was on your birthday, Mañuco, when you turned six or thereabouts, and it has been a long time

since then and now she's all grown up and I'm not exactly sure
if it was the same Adriana, but I believe it was her, because her
parents hadn't changed that much. I, speechless as hell. Then
Pocho arrived saying there was going to be a party that Saturday at the Club and one had to go in a suit and all that bullshit,
but the dance was with an orchestra which promised a lot, so
who was going to go with me. Count me in, Rudy the Tank
said, and, me, too, said Mañuco the Dog, Quarter Tango, and
Monkey Castrejon. And what about you, Tito?, are you coming
with us? wake up, Tito! Where the fuck is your brain off to?

Of course I went to the party, and all decked to the nines
and all that bullshit, hating the bullshit, of course, because I
could strangle the guy who invented these yokes they call ties
although that was the only way to get into the party that we
were invited to not coincidentally but by the ability to impress
the Club doorman to let these kids get in, because you know,
sir, we forgot our invitations, so if you want, sir, call the head of
the party, don Mauro Olaechea, just call him, call him because
he knows all of us. We went in, we always got in, and half of
Tacna was inside there because the bash was by Mr. Party Ani-
mal with enough food for an army and enough booze for the
enemy army, and an orchestra that played more frightfully than
a stomachache caused by so much booze, after all, such great
music, pal. Then I saw her, yes, I saw her and I recognized her
in the midst of that mob of people. There she was, coming towards me from afar, coming extremely beautiful and I still did
not believe it until the Dog, with all of his canine deepness told
me that's Adriana, isn't it? It was Adriana dressed in a long,
white dress as if stepping out of a movie about Greek maid-
ens to which it would be necessary to add—given its historical
context,—a glass of champagne eternally raised to the height
of her bosom.

"She's a knock out," the Dog said.

And I couldn't answer him back and I got so raging scared,
a son-of-a-bitching fear that made me tremble, sweat, speechless, and that terrified me upon seeing her there, holding her

drink, smiling at one guest, smiling at another. Anyway, it had been a century since we had seen each other, all things considered we only saw each other one time, maybe five minutes, six, shall we say a maximum of ten minutes, and I didn't know if she was going to remember my three and a half fingers' tongue, while I had spent all these years thinking about those minutes in the bathroom with you, I spent these years asking myself where you could be and I was left with only my memory and the hope that some day, I didn't know when, I didn't know in what place, I would run into you again like this, as suddenly as I ran into you the first time. And there you were and cheers for that, there you were, and you could have forgotten about the bathroom at Mañuco's house, there you were and more cheers for that.

Suddenly Adriana turned around and looked toward one side, and on that side of her life, that is, the part of the ballroom that was close to the bar, exactly on that side, there I was, me but a ten years older me, all dressed up and with all that bullshit, me scared shitless.

"Tito, that girl is checking you out," maybe it was the Dog or Mañuco. "What the hell you waiting for? Move it right now before another shark beats you to her."

I don't know if she started coming towards me but it looked like she was approaching me.

"She's coming over here, pal."

She either walked towards where I was by fluke, or who knows what, but I stopped the cheers for that and I also started to walk with my eyes searching for a sign from her eyes.

"It's been a long time, hasn't it?" I told her as we crossed each other. And silence, an instance of silence.

"Almost ten years," that sure was a significant sign.

"Do you want to dance?"

And she danced, danced, danced.

"My name is Tito."

She laughs, she laughs, she laughs. The Greek maiden dressed in white stepped out of a movie screen and she laughs,

she laughs, and she was by my side, embracing me, being embraced by me, and I feel the palm of her hand on my shoulder,
her fingers, her fingertips, her smile two and a half inches apart
from mine, her waist resting in my left hand.

"I thought you were a mute. Seriously, I thought you
couldn't speak, and that's why I wanted to prove that you had
a tongue."

"It measures three and a half fingers, Adriana."

"It must have grown in all this time," she said.

"I suppose, I don't know, I haven't bothered to measure it
again but don't ask me to show it to you now to bring its dimensions up to date, don't ask me now in the middle of twenty
thousand people."

She didn't ask me for anything, luckily, but she said that she
already knew my name, I have known that your name is Tito
for almost ten years. I got a look on my face indicating how
do you know if I never opened this mouth, and if I opened it I
never let out a word except for, Ciao! Well, she said, the truth is
that I asked my neighbor Mañuco Morales... and I thought: this
asshole Mañuco never told me anything even while we played
in front of the sky blue house. And I understood, of course I
understood, I understood that Adriana also had a memory and
I told her, let's leave, let's get out of here, let's escape from
this herd of people, and she said yes, but that we had to return
quickly because her dad was coming early to pick her up. And
we left leaving the Club behind us and we walked down San
Martin Street, the two of us, only the two of us, under a modest
wintry drizzle that was the accomplice to our first walk, while
I asked her where she had been all this time, Adriana. Then she
told me that these years had been difficult for her family, because after the coup on Velasco her father found out that he was
going to be incarcerated for having been the prefect to Tacna
during the Belaunde era and one night they had to leave their
house and they succeeded in crossing the border because her
father still had police friends. They spent only a little time in
Chile, because her father was always getting himself into a bind

there, and so Adriana's father said they had to flee from there also before the shit hit the fan, and he picked up the family and the little savings that they had left and he insisted upon moving to Caracas where there was a lot of oil and all that shit.

"Did you live in Venezuela all these years, Adriana?"

Almost all of them and there she learned how to eat and make *arepas*, a bread made from pre-cooked cornmeal, that are mouthwatering, you know, stuffed with cheese, with ham or with tuna fish, finger-licking good.

"Better than *picante de mondongo*, Adriana?"

Well, it was different, but some day I'll make *arepas* and I'll invite you over to eat, okay? My old man knew how to work it in Caracas, he made money and he learned how to save, and he believed his luck with oil wouldn't last, so when he found out Velasco had been defeated he told the family to pack our bags because we were all going back home, and we all returned a couple of years ago to live in Arequipa. Damn, I thought, Adriana has been living close by, just five hours by car, four if one puts the lead to the metal, and I like a real dumbshit asking about her everywhere. Yes, in Arequipa, she said, because her dad got a deal of a job there, but you know, my dad is from here, so one day he told us again, let's pack our bags because we're going back, because everyone goes back to where they were born, and so, here we are, here I am. What time is it, Tito? I told her what time it was and she told me it was already late and her old man would be at the Club looking for her everywhere. We made the trek back by the same route, under the same drizzle, and when we got to the Club we ran into her father at the door. Then she kissed me on the cheek, call me, she said, at 3050, so you can tell me what you did all these years, and she left without hearing my reply, because after all, all I had done in all these years was to dream about this moment.

Monday, two days after that memorable Saturday. Monday, 8:30 in the morning, and like all Mondays at that time, general assembly of all the student body in the main patio of the schoolyard. SECTION, ATTENTION! There were the little ones from elementary school and us and the school priest giving his weekly speech. SECTION, AT EASE!, and Grover, of course, Tacnean as hell, more Tacnean than *picante de mondongo*, and Miss Maru who had other kids who she also undoubtedly loved equally. The priest had already finished his weekly chatter, and the Brigadier General, Pocho that is, at full voice, ATTENTION!, because they were going to hoist the flag and play the national anthem, *we are free, may we always be so....,* and Monkey Castrejon, hey, Tito, how did it go with the chick? *...let the sun rather deny its light...* And the Dog also, Just tell us, pal, did you score with her or not? *...that we should fail the solemn vow which our country raised to God...* And Mañuco and Quarter Tango and Rudy the Tank also, all with the same line, speak, already, dumbshit, stop singing the national anthem and speak, did you do it or not? *...for a long time the Peruvian, oppressed....* Adriana's old man was super-mad, Tito, saying, who has my daughter gone out with, who did she leave with? *...but as soon as the sacred cry...* Okay, already, pal, spit it out, why is this chick so great, okay? *...we are free, let us always be so...* This dumbshit who never sings the anthem and today he becomes the ultimate patriot. *...which our country raised to God, which our country raised to God...* or did you chicken out, Tito, huh? Shut up, you Monkey shithead! SECTION, BREAK RANK! Pocho shouting, of course, and at full force.

That Monday they spent all day asking me, everybody asking me except Ortega son who, something unbelievable for him, had not been in class for three or four days. Me, silent, silent, this dream is mine, mine alone and let me continue dreaming, and to keep on dreaming when I got home I grabbed the telephone, 3050, hello, Adriana, yes, it's me, of course, it's me, Tito, yeah, I had a good time too. Your father? oh! well, well, no, it's just that... well, I... I wanted to tell you about my last ten years, since I saw you in the bathroom until I saw you again in the ballroom, now?, right now?, okay, okay, I'll come by your house, is it the same sky blue house? oh!, it's another one, then give me your address, ciao!

My old man was taking his nap, bad for him and good for me, so I took his car without his realizing it while surely he was dreaming that Bolo was the champion of the Libertadores Cup with two head goals made by his son, because, that's my son, damn. And his son, or me, that is, was at Adriana's house, picking up Adriana, riding around in the car with her, parking on the outskirts of the city, close to some vilca trees that provided enough shade for two adolescents to hide from the world, so that we could encounter the new dimensions of our tongues during a long, prolonged and infinite instant. I felt like the chosen man on this planet, and upon separating from Adriana's tongue I looked in the rearview mirror and I felt doubly chosen: half a dozen tanks were approaching with the fierceness of a shark on an ambush. Yes, tanks, tanks, just as it sounds and as it reads, TANKS, with a cannon and tank wheels and tank irons. And I said to myself what the hell is going on here, if we weren't close to patriotic festivals nor Tacnean festivals which is when the army comes out to parade and impress people and everyone stands there with their mouths wide open, including the school priest who automatically revs up his Our Father, who art in Heaven, please don't let there be war here on Earth. Before I could start the car and tell Adriana, look, baby, don't get nervous, but there is a chain of tanks shitting around, shitting around behind us, and before I could say that, two soldiers were pointing their guns at us through the windows and ordering us to get out, and she and I scared shitless in the blink of an eye. I wanted to sing the national anthem like I had done that morning, for solidarity to the country and because they say music tames beasts, but this pair of Privates didn't look like the type that would understand a lot so I defended myself saying, calm down, dote, just calm down. Adriana didn't understand it either, a soldier was pointing a gun at her and she saw the half dozen tanks that were almost on top of us. Your documents, one soldier said. I don't have any, and neither does she. You must be spies, the other one said. Spies?, Adriana and I kept wondering what the hell was happening here until suddenly a

soldier with military stripes arrived. We found these two, Lieutenant Sir, and they don't have papers. What were you two doing here?, the Lieutenant soldier asked. Adriana and I looked at
each other while they kept pointing their guns at us and then I,
scared shitless and more so, really peeing in my pants because
the soldier was rubbing my ribs with his machine gun, I told
the Lieutenant that she and I were here, under the vilca trees,
because it had been ten years, even though you may not believe
it, we have known the exact measurement of our tongues for
ten years, mine was three and a half fingers, and hers was exactly three fingers, but that we had never, never, made out, not
even once, just like you are hearing it, and that's why we came
to this shady spot, to get our first kiss, damn full of saliva, and
you with your little gang and your tanks just screwed up the
kiss of our lives, do you understand, Lieutenant, Sir? What's
this snotty-nosed kid talking about? the Lieutenant said. Take
them as prisoners of war. What war, Lieutenant? The one we
are going to start in fifteen minutes, because first we are going to attack Arica and then the rest of Chile. Holy Shit, this is
craziness! If I say crazy, it's understated, because those soldiers
were loony in the head, and even loonier was Ortega father
who was the one ordering all this nonsense and he was riding
around the streets of Tacna in a jeep with a loudspeaker in his
hand and saying that we were going to regain the territories
lost in the Pacific War, that is, a good while back, even before
my great-great grandfather had banged my great-great grandmother under the shade of a vilca tree, of course. Days later I
understood why Ortega son had missed classes and he continued missing forever more: his old man had sent the entire family out of Tacna, while he commanded the troops to approach
the border and he went around in his jeep, loony as a bird and
with his loudspeaker, shouting that he was going to recover the
saltpeter mines even though they didn't have a frickin' gram
of saltpeter. My old man was also crazy as hell because he had
just awakened tasting the victory of Bolo in the Libertadores
Cup with his son's two goals, he realized that neither his car nor

his son was there. And he went even crazier when my mother, without her smile that traverses the sky and a gigantic concern that only mothers can have for their children, hung up the telephone terrorized, dreadfully terrorized, because Mrs. Amanda had called to tell her, there's a war, there's a war, while Daniel, her son, advised everyone seriously that they should take refuge in their basements, and someone in his house answered him, Yeah, dumbshit, who builds houses in Tacna with basements? And my mother, terrified, dreadfully terrified, thanked Mrs. Amanda because she didn't know what else to tell her, and she hung up the telephone, walked over to the winder, closing the curtains slightly: soldiers were marching through the streets, and then she looked for my old man who was walking around nuts because he couldn't find his car, and my mother, terrified, dreadfully terrified, told him, there's a war, there's a war and our son is outside, and of course, for the first time in his life my father didn't have an answer and he was scared as hell. At that instant Adriana's father called asking if his daughter was there because she had left home hours ago, before the army began to mobilize in the streets, before the situation turned fire ant red, and they didn't know anything about her, absolutely nothing, except that she had been seen leaving with me in my father's car. Once again my old man was able to come up with an answer in life: I'm going to go look for them right now, and together with my mother they went out in the middle of that military hoard directly to the military general headquarters.

And my father must have missed my scent because after the Lieutenant said take them as prisoners, they put us in a jeep and we went through almost half of Tacna until we arrived at the military headquarters where another soldier took us to a small cell which he locked with two turns of a key and he commanded us to keep silent. Everything was extremely dark, and although it might sound obvious to say, we were the only prisoners of war. Adriana continued to be scared to death and she glued herself to me seeking security as if I were some type of anti-nervous breakdown pill. To be honest, I was glued to Adri-

ana as if she were an entire bottle of anti-nervous breakdown
pills. And so, well-pressed together and in silence, we stayed
there for a long time, as if we were that little girl who locks
herself up in the bathroom, hugging her stuffed rabbit, without
any possibility of opening the door and hoping that someone
from outside would come for her. That was how we were when
the same soldier reappeared who had locked the door with two
turns of a key, except that this time he turned them the other
way and both Adriana and I released our respective stuffed rab-
bits. Someone is here for you, the soldier said. My mother was
outside and upon seeing me alive and kicking she got back her
cloudlike smile that traverses the sky, and my father, of course,
who immediately yelled, that's my son, damn, that's my son,
and both of them hugged Adriana as though they were checking that everything on her was in the right place. The two of
us breathed more deeply than we had ever done before, nevertheless and in the meantime, Ortega father showed up to stop
the deep breathing and he made the mistake of saying that this
time, and only this time, he would let us go, but you, and he
pointed his index finger right into my father's nose, you need
to learn how to rear your children or the army will teach you
how. My father has always been patient—except for when Bolo
is losing—but with patience and everything he has never tolerated anyone sticking his index finger in his face, because he
knows, even with all that patience, exactly what a good right
hook is, like the one that he planted on Ortega father and that
knocked him belly up like a butterfly with its little wings up and
his ass on the floor. The soldiers stood there paralyzed because
they already knew my father and there was no messing with
that man when he was mad. Then my father went over to where
Ortega was laying and told him very clearly, that punch was
for locking up his son and his girl believing that they could be
prisoners of war, because he had to be some damn asshole to
think that, and that punch was also for the scandal of the war
that he was creating and that for sure, more than sure, when
they began to lose the war, you, Ortega, precisely you, will be

the first to take off running. My father said, Let's go! and for the first time in this story I didn't contradict him and I told Adriana, See, that's my old man. At that moment, Ortega father pulled his ass up off the floor, he adjusted his clothing, and he shouted at the soldiers to detain my father. No one moved and we all went home, and my old man forgot that I had taken his car because when he realized that I had been with Adriana surely he thought, damn, that's my son.

It must have been the school priest's prayers, or what it might have been, what else could it have been, but the tanks didn't cross the border, they stayed there, on the border, waiting for the order to move forward, the order that never came because only one voice was heard telling them to return to their barracks. That was Ortega father's war that caused his immediate transfer (a few days later he left Tacna to I don't know where, minus two teeth as a result of the wound acquired on the battlefield, that is, my father's right hook), that was the war that made all Tacneans' hair stand on end because if there was anything we didn't want it was more war, and it was also the war whose only results were two prisoners, Adriana and me, which is another way of saying that that little war interrupted the kiss of the whole story of my humanity.

Anyway, Adriana kissed me again with all her heart, her life and she told me that she was proud of the way that I had confronted that Lieutenant. I puffed up like a peacock and I felt like Coronal Bolognesi when he was already a really old man and dang sickly—or maybe that's why—he said he was going to fight until the bitter end. I didn't tell her that my legs were shaking while I was talking to the Lieutenant, because in the history books no one knows when heroes tremble. We detached our tongues and I told her, look, Adriana, Rudy the Tank wants to have a party this weekend, from war to wild bash, that's the life of a hero who is proud to be Peruvian, and I am happy, and Rudy *the Tank* says this party will be to celebrate our return from the dark prisons, you'll come, won't you?

"I'm not sure."

"Why not"?

"It's because with what happened my father is a little worried, and you know what happened hasn't been that far away, but I'll call you, I'll call you if I convince my dad, okay?"

She didn't call the next day, nor the next, nor the next either. It was Friday and Rudy the Tank told me that the bash was already planned, the music, the booze, the women, everything ready, pal, you already invited Adriana, didn't you? Then I told him that I didn't know what was going on because she had promised to call me, but nothing, Tank, nothing, and every time I called her house she wasn't there and she hadn't returned my phone calls not even by coincidence. I don't understand, Tank. A few days ago we engaged in the kiss of the century, and now it seems she wouldn't know me not even if I was in a dog fight. That's it, brother, but let's have the bash anyway, with Adriana or without her, let's have the bash anyway. That afternoon I went straight to her house and she answered the door and begged forgiveness for not having called me, but you know, Tito, I think we have to talk. We had a hell of a talk! She jumped right into telling me that after living in Venezuela they had gone to Arequipa, don't you remember I told you that? Well, they were there in Arequipa for a couple of years and then... it's that I wanted to talk to you about this before but I couldn't, I was so happy with you and I couldn't, but the truth is, Tito, is that in Arequipa I met a boy, he's a good guy and he's even already studying at the university, and he and I have been going out together, and the other day I told Adolfo—that's his name—that there was an attempted war and he got very worried and he told me that he was going to come to Tacna this weekend to see if I was okay, and that's why, well, that's why I can't go to Rudy's party with you.

I grew silent again and thought, shit, the fall of a hero, or maybe, a four-day hero, because I felt a celestial earthquake and that God and his angels, apostles and other bureaucrats came crashing down upon me, falling on my face, my chest, my stomach... in short, my whole body ached at that moment.

Adriana was probably asking me to say something, but I don't know. I lost all sound and the movie froze: her dear face there, in the foreground, with a gesture that seemed to show a wrinkle on her heart. And I, turned into even more of a frozen dumbshit until by some magical trick, I left her house without saying, Ciao! Then I told Rudy the Tank, no simple party at home, let's go get drunk in Bolognesi Park. And we all went there and we prepared a concoction of rum, vodka, the rot-gut liquor *pisco*, and a little Coca Cola, because Coca Cola makes everything worse, and the mandatory twist of lime, and with that concoction we would bathe our insides. In a short time we were magnificently plastered, and Quarter Tango, who had assessed my situation began to sing—I followed along in a duet, and then everyone joined in chorus—about what the world is and that it will be worthless and that's why I drink and I'm constrained, son of a bitch. The last drop of our concoction ran out and then Mañuco said, let's go get some whores! and that's where we went, first taxi stand, obviously, how much is it to the bordello, man, five Peruvian *soles*, okay! let's go, and haul ass, man, because we are horny as hell. We arrived at the bordello, on the outskirts of the city, or the outskirts of the valley, there on the slopes of a hill, in the middle of a sandy area where you can see one tiny light that screams out here's where the whores are. We all stuck out our chests and lit a cigarette to make us look two years older and they let us go in, and once inside we took the first right around some half-open doors, choosing the one whose legs we were going to spread. That night I got it on with black Vanessa, the one to whom I had lost my virginity not long ago, and to whom I had said, girl, teach me everything you know, and she paid perfect attention and practically left me brain dead. I didn't stay there, of course not, I went into Room 14, and then 16, to 12, to 3, a couple of rums at the bar, to 18, to 15, another couple of rums at the bar, and then again with black Vanessa who ended up totally wiping me out and she didn't leave any of my neurons intact because upon leaving

her room I told her that I loved Adriana like a son of a bitch but
the world was like that, it was worthless, and I left there, I left
the bordello, while all my friends asked me what was wrong,
Tito, and Quarter Tango kept singing the tango *Cambalache*. I
didn't get very far: I walked a few steps from the bordello door
and Kerplunk! I landed with my snout in the sand. Then I got
up and I took off my shoes and before they could stop me I told
them that I would walk barefoot the rest of my life even if my
wounds hurt more because walker there is no road in this world
that isn't and won't be worthless, and Kerplunk! snout in the
sand. There was a third Kerplunk! until they pushed me into a
taxi, and when the driver asked, Where to, youngsters, I told
him to Adriana's house, dumbshit me, because I love her like a
son of a bitch although the world is and will always be worthless. The Tank told him where we were going, the taxi driver
started the car, took off flying, it was drizzling.

    The next day Quarter Tango, the Tank and Mañuco showed
up at my house and took me to Mrs. Guillermina's to get rid
of my hangover with the hair of the dog and some *ceviche*,
marinated raw fish. And between a piece of fish and a Cheers
pal, they told me to cut out the bullcrap, because that was the
same as sharpening a dull knife with a dull knife, and I should
show more respect towards the whores and that now, brother, to
come clean with them and tell them Adriana's story and to let it
out like someone who breaks loose running and let everything
out, and if I didn't want to tell, they wouldn't say anything else,
they weren't going to ask any more, because that's what friends
are for, to listen when it was necessary to listen, and to remain
silent when it was necessary to keep quiet. Then I told them
yes, that I felt like spilling my guts, because, as you know bud-
dies, the sky has fallen on me hitting me hard on all sides, from
my head to my balls, since I found out that Adriana was going
out with what's his name who lives in Arequipa, and when she
spilled her guts completely I couldn't think, I couldn't think
about anything, my only solution was to tell her, Ciao!, and
Adriana stood there with her sweet eyes shining because a mis-

chievous tear was escaping, and I, well I looked for you guys and you already know that part of the story. Rudy the Tank proposed beating the shit out of that dumbshit and that was it.

"After pounding him up, I'll land him on his stomach and I'll leave him flatter than a pancake."

Quarter Tango and Mañuco looked at each other, they looked at me and they told me that I was a dumbass to leave her like that, without even fighting for her, and in any case, in any case, brother she had already screwed this guy by being unfaithful and if that is how it had been it was because you set the little woman's hormones on fire, pal, so cut the crap, because what did it matter if one didn't go through the main door if he was always going to have an open window. They were right, damn right, so I told them that after the *ceviche* I would shoot out of there to Adriana's house and Quarter Tango warned, telling me to hold out, brother, to take it slowly, why be in such a hurry, it would be better to see her next week, being calmer and less gutsy, and you give it to her good with lots of kissing and everything you can muster up, and it would be better now, right now, to go to Professor Grover's, just plain Grover as he was known, who is looking for volunteers to visit people in jail and there we could play a nice game of basketball with the Al Capons of Tacna, does that seem like a plan to you?

And we went there. It wasn't the first time that we met with Professor Grover at the jail door on the weekend and from there we all entered together and the prisoners happy because visitors had arrived, yeah, Professor Grover's students had come, and on the way we got up a basketball game, and a basket made by Pocho from middle court. They also took out the guitar and a crate to sit on and Hiena Valdeblanca, who had been stuck inside for stealing since he was eighteen years old, and who had spent some time in Lurigancho jail, and there one is a fool, little brother, here it's just calm, so calm that when I want to escape I escape and no one realizes it, that same Hiena Valdeblanca belched out a song, *Let me tell you Tacnean girl*, and we were

glued to him because shit he sang with his heart life and soul.
Hiena Valdeblanca was luck for all of us, and he taught me how
I had to win: first, you look him in the eyes, and if the other guy
isn't very far away you hurl him a kick in the balls, and if he
bends over, he didn't do anything but crap in his pants, and on
the way you nail him with a side-kick in the face as if you were
a Korean karate master like in the movies; now, if this guy is
really close, well, that's another tune, because you should use
your head, and with one blow you break his nose and his teeth
and with that he's already more than done for. But that afternoon he didn't tell me how I should defend myself, we played a
basketball game that Professor Grover refereed, and later Hiena
told me they were finally going to take him to trial that week
because he was fed up with being stuck there without knowing if they were going to find him guilty or not, and if he was
guilty he wanted to know right then how long they were going
to sentence him to jail.

I confess that Quarter Tango's plan worked, because while
we were there I forgot about Adriana, I forgot about her boyfriend's story, I forgot about the previous night's scandal I had
caused taking my shoes off at the brothel, and falling on my
snout an infinite number of times in the sandy dessert. But the
plan only worked for a while because upon leaving the jail I
remembered everything and then I left the group and told my
friends, Ciao! see you later Professor Grover, and I went straight
to Adriana's house. Her boyfriend wasn't there. He was staying
with his aunt and uncle at a house they had in Tacna, and of course,
she and I were left alone, and I begged her to forgive me, to
forgive me for not having said anything the other day, for being such an asshole, and Adriana, of course, she forgave me,
although truthfully, Tito, there is nothing to forgive, and I got
a look on my face like a flower blossoming in the springtime,
and then I lost my words and Wham! I searched for her three-
finger tongue with my three and a half-finger tongue, and since
that time and for a good while, I went to Adriana's house while
her boyfriend hung out at the university, and I disappeared with

my friends when her boyfriend left the university and showed up in Tacna walking around with an added inch of cuckolded infidelity.

That's how the last year of high school went by, that last year in which Professor Grover told us that we had to go to an academy in Lima where they would prepare us for the university entrance exam, and please, Professor Grover said, those of you who have your little sweethearts here, start breaking it off with them, because writing love letters takes time and then the girl doesn't write back and later you start thinking that maybe your girlfriend is cheating on you, and that's where the worrying begins. Did she leave me for another? Doesn't she love me anymore? And so no one can concentrate on his studies, boys, and no one passes his university entrance exam, so please, forget your sweetheart in Tacna, study all summer, and when you get to the university find another sweetie there, and that's it, everyone's happy. That was how Grover was, and who knows why he was named Grover.

So the year went by, it was December, at the beginning of December, and we all already knew what academy and what boarding house we would go to in Lima, I would go to 820 Leon Velarde, in the Lince section of Lima, to Miss Blanca's boarding house, Quarter Tango was going to the same boarding house, Pocho was going to his uncle's who lived in Callao, Mañuco was still not sure. And so the year went by, and Adriana and I spent the year better than good, while her boyfriend's cuckold horns grew longer, although at times we got worried, yes, the worry that I would be packing for Lima soon, because my crazy dreams were going to take me from my home, and then we would no longer see each other every day, of course, Adriana had to stay in Tacna to finish her last year of high school but occasionally she could take a little trip to Lima and once in a while I could take a little trip to Tacna to see her. And that very afternoon we promised each other that we would see each other and look for each other all our lives, and we sealed our promise with an infinite kiss, and one day we will have children, Adriana told me.

"Yes, of course."

"And what shall we name our first born?"

"I don't know, Adriana. What do you want to name him?"

"I don't know either."

"How about…?"

"Okay, tell me."

"How about… Rudy?" I said.

"Rudy? Why Rudy?"

"Maybe because he offered to be the best man at our wedding."

"Really?"

"Yes. And I don't know… He has always paid attention to everything and taken care of me in everything. He says he is going to apply to San Marcos University, and I believe that he is thinking about doing it because I want to go to that university."

"Okay, then let's name him Rudy. Besides, I don't know. I like the name Rudy, and I like Rudy. And if it's a girl?"

"We'll call her Rude."

"Tito!"

"Honestly, I don't know, Adriana."

"And our second son?"

That's what we were up to, me giving her another infinite kiss to seal the pact of the name of our first son when suddenly, life surprises you, life surprises you, Adolfo himself appeared without an invitation or anything, the cuckolded boyfriend, and he found us in full action and the shit hit the fan. Who knows how someone comes to find out about the goings on! But I was convinced it was his cousin, the one who lives here in Tacna, a little past Zela Square, who told him the gossip. Because he could have seen us one afternoon walking together down San Martin Street, sitting on a bench in Zela Square, eating ice cream that melted on the spot and that left our hands and face sticky grime. Maybe Adolfo's cousin had seen us there, maybe that's how Adolfo himself found out, and surely he felt cuckolded written all across his forehead and he forgot that he had classes at the university, he forgot about being a model and impeccable student and he took the first bus from Arequipa to Tacna and for the six-hour crossing of the desert he grumbled over the weight of her cheating, grumbled how Adriana could have done this to him, planning how he was going to knock the shit out of the person who had gotten involved with her, and the desert continued, it continued infinitely, and Adolfo kept tearing the unfortunate guy to shreds who had made him the butt of this cuckolding. Adriana was the first to see him and she separated herself from me automatically but it was already late, too late, we had kissed for twenty-seven minutes fourteen seconds and two-tenths of a second and Adolfo had seen at least the last part. He came straight towards me, mumbled something, something like that was how he wanted to find us and I remembered Hiena Valdeblanca's lessons. If your opponent is far away, a kick in the balls, Hiena told me; if he's close, a bash with your head in the middle of his nose. Adolfo was still a little bit away when I saw him with a total wish to rip my soul apart and I decided to kick him in the balls and the shameless guy grabbed my foot and there with one foot in the air I thought about Hiena Valdeblanca who hadn't told me what the hell to do in this type of situation. I didn't think much though. I didn't have time because the cheating woman's boyfriend raised my leg towards the sky and I ended up flying, and when I tried to get up to smack him with my head he landed another kick that sent me to the ground again, and we went on like that for a good while, me trying to get up and the wretch with bare kicks between my ribs and my stomach until suddenly Adriana burst into tears and she told him to leave me alone, please, enough, leave him alone, Adolfo, and I was happy because she was crying for me even though it was my ribs that were being shattered. Then Adriana's father arrived and he clobbered Adolfo a couple of times which left him paralyzed and he asked him why he was thrashing me. Adolfo couldn't answer, he wasn't able to get out, sir, you know, I'm the cheating girl's boyfriend, and you

know, sir, your daughter has been cheating on me on purpose
with this guy who is still a snot-nosed kid in high school.

Adolfo couldn't say anything, and Adriana kept crying and
crying, while I was trying to count the ribs that were still intact.
Adriana's father asked me how I was doing, and I told him
that I was just a little bruised, but still alive and kicking. Good,
her father said, it's better for you to go home, and you Adolfo,
go to your aunt and uncle's house. Tomorrow you'll both be
calmer. But Adriana stayed there, crying and crying, and at that
moment I didn't understand why there was such a waterfall of
tears if the fight was already over. Then she approached me and
she asked me to forgive her, please, to forgive her, she had not
wanted for all of this to happen, and I told her that there was
no problem, Adriana, a patch on my ribs and that was it. And
she also asked me to forgive her for what she was about to say,
yes, please, because when she saw Adolfo as furious as he was,
coming from Arequipa to here just for her, jealous because of
her, leaving his studies, his classes, leaving everything for her,
she had realized the he loved her, that he must love her a lot,
and she also realized that she loved him and it wasn't fair that
she was cheating on him, it wasn't fair to deceive anyone and
even less fair to do it to a person who one loves, and to forgive
her because she couldn't go on like this, Tito, and you, Adolfo,
forgive me for this also, and I refused to hear any more, I only
saw that she hugged the son of a bitch of a cheating woman, and
I thought that twenty minutes ago we had promised each other
to look for each other all of our lives, to love each other all of
our lives and before you can say Jack Robinson that promise
ended up as waste in the trashcan and it was a pity that Quarter
Tango was not here because he would have sung *today, today
an oath, tomorrow a treason, student loves are flowers for one
day because the world is and will be worthless*. Then I made a
180 degree turn in the opposite direction of Adriana being held
by her cuckolded boyfriend, and from her father who didn't
know which instrument to play at this dance. As I walked I felt
a bitter taste in my mouth, a taste of rotten fruit that invaded

my teeth, my tongue, my palate and the more I spit and spit the taste still wouldn't go away. I wanted to remember Quarter Tango's advice, if you don't enter through the door, go in through the window, but this time, my dear friend, this time they had bolted the window from inside. Then, as I was trying to get that taste out of my mouth, I prayed to God, I begged Señor de Locumba, miracle worker capable of all things impossible, I begged him to speed time up so that December would go one hundred miles an hour, one hundred and twenty would be even better, one hundred and fifty still better, so that soon, very soon, I could pack my bags taking the very best of my own things and myself, leaving what I had to leave, crossing the desert from Tacna to Lima in search of a future, because that's my son, who is going to study at the university, in search of a future where all truths could be reality, except for Adriana who had closed the doors, the windows and even the last corner through which I could reach her.

A Story of Moves

* * *

A ll of us, well, almost all of us, got into the university. Some in Lima, others in Arequipa, and a few in Tacna. Miss Goalie, of course, stayed behind kicking cans, but during the summer months he met a girl who was more of a space cadet than him the poor thing, or maybe even more ditzy than him the poor thing, who wasn't even able to take advantage of what they call beginner's luck. Neither one of them understood an algebraic formula or what is known as verbal reasoning, but during those months they discovered sex and they spent the summer screwing and mega screwing, and of course, Professor Grover probably thought, anything but passing an entrance exam. But that's not all, Professor Grover, because Miss Goalie messed things up, he messed things up so foolishly and he was able of confusing the most sacred parts of life and this time, Professor Grover, this time he confused the use of a condom with contraceptives and then he took the pill and he put it on the end of his penis, and the major idiot later confessed that it hurt him, that little pill hurt me like hell, pal, and so the summer went by, every evening, every night, putting the pill on himself to prevent pregnancy and before the summer was over Miss Goalie's girlfriend—Tencha was her name, and still is her name—ended up expecting a child and the two of them, a pair of morons, wondered why, why if we have been using a contraceptive pill. So Miss Goalie was the first to have an offspring (Rudy the Tank was the godfather at the baptism) and they got married like the law requires, first in a civil ceremony and later in a mass at church that the same priest who was the principal of the school performed.

It was the period in which the last Viceroy of Peru had returned from his political exile with all his court to present himself as a candidate for president because about twelve years

had already gone by since the last elections and voting was
going to be a great novelty for some. That was what Adriana's
father thought also since he was a candidate for representative
in the same party (or the same court), although he had reserva-
tions that he would confess to me many years later, yes, because Adriana's father told the Viceroy that in Ayacucho an
underground movement was being organized, Mr. President, a
movement that might end peace in the country because of the
destruction of the blockheads is only a sign, Mr. President, and
if we don't chop it off at the root now, later it will be very difficult. The Viceroy looked at him showing a life time calmness
like a former democratic president that we had, that problems
resolve themselves or they don't resolve themselves, Mr. Representative. I am concerned about establishing a waterway route
between the Amazon and the Orinoco Rivers which would be
extremely important for South American unity, don't you think
so? Because take note that here, on this map, the Orinoco is in
these surroundings and I am thinking about speaking with the
Navy to take a small trip from the Amazon River up to there.
Can you imagine us discovering the Fountain of Youth on the
way? It wouldn't be bad for me since I'm already somewhat
old!

"But, Sir, there is a terrorist movement emerging in our
country."

"My dear Representative, I don't believe there is any terrorism in the Orinoco River."

Obviously, the last Viceroy of Peru and Adriana's father
ended up being elected, and none of us voted for them except
Miss Goalie who did it by mistake, while Rudy the Tank voided
his vote saying that this country deserved better candidates. By
that time I had already started at the university. Law at San
Marcos University, and I spent all summer living in a small
room (Quarter Tango was in the room next door) at 820 Leon
Velarde, a boarding house for Tacnean students run by Miss
Blanca, a Tacnean, who was around sixty something and since
she had no children not even illicitly she adopted all the univer-

sity students. There I reacquainted myself with some of my old classmates from school who had already been at the university for two or three years: Colorado Gil who had popped the question and was engaged with a ring on his ring finger and everything, who would go abroad shortly, already married, of course, already with two children, of course. Marciano shared a room with Colorado, although better than Marciano, which means Martian, they should have baptized him as Lunatic, because he walked around as if he were on the moon and dreaming, so one day he would say, yesterday I was closing a business deal in Paris and tomorrow I'm going to sign a contract of sale and purchase in New York, and therefore, maybe because of that, he applied to the diplomatic corps, and because of that, maybe also because of that, he was rejected faster than immediately, and later after some time in life the only thing left for him to say was, yesterday I closed a deal in Pocollay (a town a little over a mile from Tacna). Tomorrow I will travel to Sama (another town close to Tacna), and then he'd stick his chest out, he'd swell up and he'd feel important. And he shared a room on the first floor of the boarding house with Dante and the Blind Man, who not only all shared a room, but also sweaters, shirts, dress pants, a pair of Wrangler blue jeans, Adidas shoes that were about fifteen years out of style, a Lacoste shirt, they shared everything but their underwear, because that's perverted, man.

I had been living at the boarding house for a little over three months, I would have a little more time living there and I would always remember,—I will always remember—the afternoon that I left Tacna for Lima, the afternoon that my mother with her cloud-like smile that traverses a sunny sky, was arranging each shirt, each handkerchief, each pair of socks in my suitcase as if she were giving me a sign that I do so in an unimagined future on the way back home. My father, meanwhile, furnished me with his advice and precautions of living in the capital, because in Lima, son, you must keep your eyes wide open, you let your guard down just a bit and they'll steal your wallet, your watch, and even the sunglasses that you never use, so it's

better if you wear your watch on the right side, don't dawdle
in the street either, because in Lima there are a lot of evildoers
and in some corner they'll take out a pistol or a knife and it's
one thing to get beat up, but another to get stabbed with a knife,
so keep your eyes open, son, careful. And after everything had
been packed we went to the bus station and I gave my father
a big hug, because that's my son, damn, my mother gave me a
big kiss and I saw that her eyes couldn't hide a certain shimmer
of sadness, and only after a long time did I understand that on
that afternoon my parents already knew that from the moment
that I got on the bus to cross the desert heading towards Lima,
that from that moment my life would change, and their lives
as well. I phoned them frequently and I called them again on
the day that I started at the university and my father with telephone in hand jumped high enough to scrape the sky, he got in,
he got in!, a jump that sprained his ankle when he fell down,
but even with his twisted foot they had a party in my absence
with the tasty wine that had just aged from the Velasquez farm,
and at the boarding house we threw a party with all the people
who lived there, and Mañuco and fat Lucho and Pocho also
came straight from Callao where he was staying with his aunt
and uncle. Along the way we opened up a little rum, mixed it
with its Coca Cola and lime, a little ice, and, cheers, to the new
university student! and I was on about the fourth or fifth rum
wondering like a dumbshit if Adriana was around here.

At the end Quarter Tango, Mañuco and I were left, and in a
while, not much longer afterwards, Quarter Tango fell asleep on
the dining room table and that's when Mañuco told me that he
had been screwed ever since he arrived in Lima. First because
he was staying at his aunt and uncle's place and the truth is,
brother, they turned out to be a pair of hotheads who only waited
for his old man to send the monthly check for his boarding fee.
His cousin Julia was cool, but she wasn't the owner and her old
man acted as though he had disinherited her since she decided
to become a single mother. So after a month and a half Mañuco
took off flying from his aunt and uncle's house to a boarding

house that his cousin Julia graciously found for him, but things went from bad to worse, brother, because he was living with a couple of crazy ladies, crazy, more than crazy, and the other night the boyfriend of one of them left her and the crazy woman was throwing glasses and plates and then she went in her room to get drunk alone. But it didn't stop there, Tito, she went to her bedroom, and while I was completely asleep, this woman slipped into my bed, just like you are hearing it, she started on me just like someone going into a store to check out the clothing, or better said, to try on the clothing, because before I could wake up, I already had a hard on, and before I could wake up I was screwing her (or she was screwing me, without meaning that this was perverted, of course), when I woke up, I realized that I had banged that crazy woman and then I felt a general decaying that grew and exploded exactly and precisely when it occurred to her to give me a post-sex kiss. Then she told me that I must be a fag who was disgusted by women and vomited thinking about them, and to tell the truth, brother, it's one thing to be a fag and something very different to be disgusted by that crazy woman. But after all, Tito, the damn thing is, what would Professor Grover say, because nobody could concentrate like that not even to study the tables times two and I've started looking for a new boarding house.

"Move here."

"Is there room?"

"Let me speak to Mrs. Blanca."

And Mrs. Blanca didn't have any buts for Mañuco to move to my room for a while and later he could go to live in Colorado Gil's room who by that time had gotten married to his lifetime girlfriend. That's it, she said, I'll show it to you, you'll have to share Colorado's room with Marciano who turns more lunatic daily and how he's going around saying that next month he's leaving on a Caribbean cruise.

That same weekend Mañuco moved and I went to the boarding house where he was living to lend him a hand. He didn't have a lot of things—none of us had much—some books, one suitcase of clothes, a box with the rest of the junk that one always ends up accumulating. Then his cousin Julia arrived in her car to give us a ride, and that was the first time I saw her and she seemed damn fine, with her thirty-some years she was well preserved and I bet a lot of fifteen year old debutants would have liked to have the body that she wielded. Later I found out that she was an aerobics teacher and then I understood a little, and that a few years back that she ended up pregnant almost by some type of magic art because no one knew of any definite sweetheart, nor did she have the reputation of being slutty, she just ended up pregnant and she told her parents that she was going to have a child without a father, and her old man called her a whore and all its implications and he kicked her out of the house, and Julia told him she was leaving and she also told him that yes, she was a whore with all its implications but no one could take away her right to be a mother, and so she was leaving, and she went straight to her room, opened her suitcase which hadn't been used since its arrival at the train station at Peru and she threw everything in that she found without any order. Her mother interceded, she let loose in front of the old man and in front of her, surely she said something like, my dear daughter, boo, hoo, hoo—the mom crying -, daughter, don't go, and well, finally, Julia and her dad hugged each other, they let out of couple of boo hoos also, and the soap opera was solved and she decided to stay at her own home. Months later the company came. She named her Maria Lucero and when I met her she was about to turn one year old, and she was starting to say her first words and one of them was my name, Tito. It's not very complicated, of course, only when she said Tito the first time we all celebrated and then Maria Lucero repeated again Tito Tito Tito and I was happy as life. If she wanted her bottle, she would say Tito Tito, her rattle, Tito Tito, when her diaper was wet, Tito Tito, when she poopied, Tito Tito.

But it was on the very same afternoon that Mañuco moved to the boarding house that Mañuco came out with the news that he had decided to apply for the Navy. Well, he would apply at the Catholic University also, but he thought he would give priority to the Navy. I looked at him from our childhood until the present and I told him, how long have you been interested in the damn service, or do you think life at sea is more pleasing? Mañuco turned serious and deep. But damn serious and damn deep, more than the Dog in his undertakings of immeasurable deepness. I have thought about it carefully, he told me, while I scratched an ear without understanding what insect had bitten it, or perhaps, was it maybe the romp in the hay with that old lady that had traumatized him to the point of thinking about such nonsense for his future?

"No, no," he told me, "I've been thinking about it carefully for the last two years of high school."

"Yeah, yeah," I said. "You've thought about it at every binge we pulled on Bolognesi Avenue?"

He always knew that I had developed a phobia against the military because we were up against them all during our childhood, adolescence and to make matters even worse the military had carried out a coup d'état during the kiss of my life when Adriana and I were under the pleasant shade of the vilca trees, and now, now that the military had disappeared after they had invented inflation, now that they no longer even showed up on television and they would be embarrassed up to their boots for a long time and at least they would respect the elections, now that all of this is happening my friend Mañuco tells me that he has considered it carefully and that he's going to be the last version of the knight of the seas.

"Yes, yes, I've thought about it carefully and meticulously, and I am as interested in the Navy as you are with the phobia that you have against the military and that doesn't surprise me, you know, because I've also thought about that carefully and meticulously."

Then he indicates that the two of us are like the two sides of the same coin, or better said, pal, like an image that one sees in a mirror that is always identical and always the opposite, and that's why I don't find it strange that you and I have completely opposing opinions, because what I am telling you is also cautiously and meticulously thought out.

I don't know where he pulled that mirror story out of but I confess that it threw me off guard and at that moment it wasn't him but rather me who wanted to be Popeye the Sailorman looking for love in every port (although the latter thought was more intriguing), so I told him that I hope they give you one hell of a ship to toast you on the open sea accompanied by a pair of sirens who we screw meticulously.

I don't know it if was my intuition, but I kept hoping that they would accept Mañuco at the Catholic University and that he would forget that life at sea was more pleasing. And Mañuco got into the Catholic University, even in the first round, and I told him, see, you are too intelligent to be a military. Then he answered me back, heh, heh, heh, son of a bitch, heh heh, and a week later he was accepted at the Naval Academy and the following week he had to leave the boarding house to go live there where life is more pleasing. So another move again, the box of books again, the suitcase, the bag and nothing more, Julia in her car again and the three of us left and Mañuco stayed behind (he stayed for two months without leaving the Academy), and Julia and I returned and then she confessed to me that her cousin seemed like a nice person, it was a pity he hadn't accepted to study at the Catholic University instead of entering the Navy.

"I think so also," I said, "but everyone is master of his own life."

"You're right."

And she sat there astoundingly thoughtful as if I had said something deep. And I never said jackshit deep, that is the Dog in this story, all I ever said was pure bullshit.

"You're right," she said again after half an hour driving in her Hundai, and there I got so worried I couldn't even swallow my own saliva.

"Right about what, Julia?"

"Oh, nothing, but I'll buy you a beer. Sound good?" And she turned as if heading for the beach.

It wasn't the first time that Julia and I had gone out to have a drink or to a café around Miraflores, or sometimes we ended up as a group dancing on some gully rock or further out in Rimac. But everything has always been as part of our party group because I was seventeen years old and she was almost twice my age and besides that she was Mañuco's cousin, although many times he had told me exactly that, Julia's not bad looking, right? Why don't you lay her, because she must be needing it? But the last reason, or the first reason, why should I hide it, is because Adriana had not disappeared even an inch from my memory. That's also how I felt when I drank the first *pisco* sour (because we weren't drinking beers but rather *pisco* shots), there in her car watching how the sun dissipated behind the sea. On the second drink I held firm in my Adrianesque framework, but by the fifth or sixth drink, it wasn't that she disappeared from my memory but that my memory began to relax and, of course, Julia's also began to relax so that by the eighth shot and with an almost patriotic endeavor she said, You're right, and I was damn worried for being the cause of being right, but I shit a brick in no time on my worries when she hurled a voracious smack with the ninth *pisco* sour while the sun, there far behind the sea, stuck out a hand saying, I'm drowning, I'm drowning, or maybe simply, until tomorrow at six. At first it was really weird because we didn't know the exact dimension of our tongues and Julia's tongue seemed a desperate confusion in my mouth because it went up down ran into a tooth went up again down up hitting against my palate and it kept on leaping until suddenly everything was as smooth as silk (we're not exaggerating either), and by this time the sun had sunken completely and then what had to happen happened. And afterwards, of course, came an infinite calmness like a meadow without any wind. For an instant we remained suspended in time, floating on the sky, holding hands. In an instant, we came down from the sky, we drank a shot while we drank from each other's smile, and then she, in a split-second, much more earthly, told me that we should go, she didn't want to arrive very late to avoid more fighting with her old man, and in nothing flat, we arrived at the boarding house and Julia kissed me good night that seemed more like a kiss to take me through the night, and she left me again floating on the sky, and later she said that I was right, and I just kept on without understanding absolutely anything about anything but floating in the sky as her car turned the corner.

When I crossed the small boarding house living room, the tremendously lunatic Marciano appeared, begging forgiveness because he had not been able to eat with all of us (really, he said to dine, in reality, we never ate together) because at the last minute he, and according to him, he had to travel to New York.

"And New York is New York, and you have to see that city, because New York is New York, with its theaters, its buildings, 42nd Avenue," and he left as if he had closed a business deal in the World Trade Center.

I continued floating in the sky while I heard someone tell Mrs. Blanca, as if it were a whisper, that every day this boy lives more on Mars and I bet you that if we ask him in English how old he is, he would answer you back because New York is New York. I went into Quarter Tango's bedroom to find him fanatically concentrated studying who the hell knows what he maintained his concentration when I flung myself on his bed, and I stayed there staring at the ceiling where a spider web was hanging.

The next day I woke up with my memory working at a hundred miles an hour, and upon opening my eyes Adriana was almost against my face, and as I bathed she appeared to hand me the soap looking toward one side she handed me the towel when I stepped out of the shower, the comb, it's about time for you to go to the barber shop, she told me, and I unwrapped the towel from around my waist to scare her, and she told me, Oh, how embarrassing! I can't see you like that! Then I put the towel back around my waist like a dumbshit and she asked me what I wanted to eat for breakfast. *Pisco*, I told her, and this time I woke up, I really work up and I pinched myself solidly to

prove that it was a dream, and that morning my breakfast was
pisco mixed in orange juice while Mrs. Blanca looked at me
extremely worried, because of course, it wasn't just one little
drink, but five straight and when I was about to drink the fifth
the dream about Adriana came to me again until I downed that
shot and everything disappeared.

After my classes I called Julia. She wasn't at home, so I
dialed her work number. She was about to leave and she told
me that she would pass by to pick me up in a few minutes. I
counted the minutes and not eight had passed by when I saw
her out of my bedroom window her car parallel parking in front
of 820 Leon Velarde. As I crossed the boarding house living
room keeping the calmness and demeanor I displayed, my
Adrianesque principles began to attack me. I speeded up my
gait and upon seeing Julia seated in her car, waiting for me
with her smile, Adriana and the dream about Adriana began to
diminish.

But that time we didn't go to the beach. Julia parked the car
close to Barranco Square and when I got out, I felt like a char-
acter in a salsa song, and I looked on one side, I looked on the
other side, and then I told her I don't know of any hotel close
to here, Julia. She tried to pinch my arm, and we kept walking
until we entered a café called Las Mesitas. Las Mesitas was not
the trendiest as far as cafes go but it wasn't bad. It had chairs
with round backs, round tables, the waiters wore a bow tie covered in a vest that made them look rounder than they probably
already were. We sat around a small table in a corner that had
been castrated to form a straight angle.

"You're right, you know," she said.

"Yes, of course."

I ordered a *pisco* sour, and Julia a coffee with a little cream
and at that instant I suspected that night (still evening) that we
weren't going to do it. Julia wrapped the coffee served in a
glass with a napkin and then she told me that sometimes poets
and artists come to this café.

"Really?"

And once she had seen Antonio Cisneros with all of his gang of young poets there and she had also seen Marco Martos, do you know who they are? "No one has ever introduced them to me, Julia."

"But have you read them?"

"Well, a little."

"If you want, one day we can go to a reading they perform at the bookstore just down the street."

"Yeah, why not?"

I didn't know it but Julia had studied literature for two years at the Catholic University. She had to drop out of the university because her father didn't want to give her money to study something which he didn't find worthwhile. So she began to work odd jobs and later she decided to take some classes at San Marcos University and there she met the poets Cisneros, Martos, and of course, she registered for a class with Cornejo Polar to study literary heterogeneity.

"Say what, Julia?"

"I'll explain it to you another time."

Then her father pops up again telling her that she was already over thirty and it was time for her to get married, and also that it was time for her to have kids because her biological clock was ticking, and what kind of life was that going around with no husband or anything at this stage in her life. She told me that everything was pure coincidence.

"Really, Tito, I didn't do it to go against my father."

But back then she went to a poetry reading at San Marcos given by a Cuban poet. The reading was damn good, the best that she had ever heard in her life, and after the whole thing there was a get together at the poet Martos' house that she was invited to.

"I was happy with the reading, and later, in Martos' house, I stood gaping at the Cuban poet who lived his own poetry. That night, well, that night we slept together, and the next day he left, and since then he has written to me a couple of times. He doesn't know it, maybe he'll never know it, but he is my daughter's father."

I didn't know whether to congratulate her for laying a Cuban poet or to tell her how sorry I was that you have a daughter without a father, or to tell her that Adriana and I never had children. Not only that, we never even had sex although I had erections for her since I was six years old. But Julia didn't give me any time to respond because from there she went on to tell the entire labyrinth of her old man who called her a whore and all that bullshit for ending up pregnant without having a husband, and after a lot of intense crying and mediation from her mother, he forgave her.

"But forgive me for what? By any chance did I commit some crime that needs forgiveness?"

"Of course not."

"Well, then… then you showed up."

"Me? Where did I show up?"

"Don't you remember?"

"I remember that last night we had one hell of a screw."

"I'm not talking about that."

"Is there anything more than that?"

"You showed up on the night that my cousin Mañuco was going to move. And I liked you from the first time you came."

"I never knew that I could impress someone so much."

"But you were seventeen years old."

"I'm still seventeen."

"I know, and that turns me on. Nevertheless, I've had enough scandals in my family to start a new one."

"What scandal, Julia? It's not like we screwed our brains out in front of everyone and no one has said anything. We had a hell of a lay and there's not a smidgen of scandal about it."

"It's because I am seventeen years older than you."

"Well, there are things in life that don't change."

"So I opted not to hit on you until that evening when we left Mañuco at the Naval Academy and everyone was his own boss, and I thought that you were right."

"Don't make me so right because it worries me."

"I love your seventeen-year old worried face."

"Then let's have another lustful fuck."

"Not now, Tito."

"Don't put off until tomorrow what you can do today."

"It's that I wanted to tell you that you were right, that I am the boss of my own life, and that I am happy to be with you although you are seventeen years younger, and because you are seventeen years younger.

"…"

"I've already finished saying what I had to say. What are you thinking about so much?

"I believe… that you are right, Julia."

"Come, get closer, and kiss me with your seventeen years."

We continued like that, me without having anything clear and she without expecting anything clearly except that I would always remain seventeen years old. Quarter Tango knew the story. I told him from the beginning and afterwards he followed it chapter by chapter (without details, of course, because I kept the details to myself). But I also had to say something to Mañuco, I wasn't sure what, maybe just tell him, you know, pal, I am involved in a phenomenal love affair with your cousin Julia. And so it was, because after two months closed up in the Naval Academy, Mañuco was set free and independent and Julia and I went to pick him up and there we found him with his frickin' exit uniform, accompanied by Ortega son who had also enlisted in the Navy because he wanted to follow in his family's footsteps.

Ortega son and Mañuco had become super chummy in the Navy. They were never friends during high school but having known each other in the past led to certain complicity—almost a brotherhood that they were sharing in the present. I hugged both of them because it felt damn good to see them again, and suddenly Ortega father showed up to pick up his son. He recognized me, of course he recognized me, but he acted as if he hadn't seen me not even in a dogfight because the whacking my old man laid upon him that landed him on his ass on the floor still hurt him. The Ortegas left and we did too, and after leaving us at the boarding house, Julia also left saying that Mañuco and I had a lot of things to talk about. Mrs. Blanca had prepared a hell of a *picante de mondongo* Tacnean style and a hell of a jerked meat disk in honor of Mañuco's return. It is very delicious, ma'am, very good, the only bad thing about the Naval Academy is that no one cooks *picante de mondongo* like this. Mañuco was happy with being Popeye the Sailorman even if he didn't have an Olive Oil. They had gotten rid of his grime by making him float on his back, frogging, running from one end to another, tolerating the water of sweat until he felt that he was almost drowning, enduring the raging cries of the serviceman on duty as if it were simply an act of nature, taking up arms of all different calibers, I have an eagle's aim, brother, cleaning the filthiest ship, hanging from the mast like a flag, all of this he had been through, and the S.O.B. happier than happy. He only looked worried when he told me that in the Academy there were rumors that a terrorist movement in Ayacucho was underway. I told him that the Minister of Internal Affairs had dispelled that story and that in fact he had discharged the Chief of Police for saying something about it.

"But it appears to be true, Tito, and we're not prepared to go up against them. And around here, what other things have been going on?"

Then I told him that his cousin and I were involved in an awesome love affair. That's it, I just let it out cold turkey, an affair that you couldn't imagine. He slapped my shoulder, so, we've gone from being friends to being family and she's the best one out of my family. We finished the spicy trip and the fried donuts with sugarcane honey that Mrs. Blanca had made and when she wasn't paying attention, Mañuco told me almost whispering, you know, brother, it's been two months since I've seen a woman, nothing but unpleasant sailors' asses taking showers, so it's a matter of life and death to go to the brothel. Want to go?

"No, brother, I'll pass. I'm faithful to Julia, and the only brothel I know in Lima is very far away."

Mañuco insisted, of course he insisted, he insisted claiming there was a mini-bus that left from University Park straight to the honeypot, without any stops or anything, and so, pal, if you want to be faithful, just don't lay anybody, take some pictures of me, and that's good enough.

But the story didn't stop there. The next weekend (now he had all his weekends free) he started the same shit again, and saying that a sailor's physical condition was in the best shape and that he needed to have a certain amount of sexual venting at least once a week, without counting a daily dose of jacking off. That was the last time I went with him and I know that sometimes he went with Ortega son and that other times he'd take a regular bus from University Park. He didn't care about anything that was going on around him because it seemed that he received orders that on Saturdays he was ordered to screw wherever he could and with whomever he could. It didn't surprise me that he arrived late at Colorado Gil's going away party and smelling like such a fifth degree slut that even Mrs. Blanca realized it. Of course, Colorado Gil had not lived at the boarding house since he married Pilar, his life-long girlfriend, but Mrs. Blanca kept on loving him as if he were her favorite son and since she found out that he had received a scholarship to complete his Masters in the United States, she wanted to organize a going away meal for him (*picante de mondongo*, of course), with all the guys at the boarding house. And so it was, she made the meal and shortly afterwards Colorado and Pilar left, and from the group of guys who all knew each other, they were the first to leave the country, because two or three years later Dante, who was already a pilot graduated from a private aviation school and with some flight time experience (according to many, transporting cocaine to the jungle), was hired by a Canadian company to fly a Boeing 721 and, of course, Dante didn't think about it twice and he shot out of there and went to live in Montreal. And who would have imagined, not even I

imagined it, nor my mother with her cloud-like smile that traverses the sky, who would have imagined at that time that I
would grab my bags and that I would also leave the country.
But all this happened later, much later. For now, the semester at
the university was ending and I was going to Tacna.

On that first return I traveled with Quarter Tango and Pocho
who had also finished their university exams. My parents were
waiting for me at the bus terminal with all the illusions of seeing their son, because that's my son, who is studying to be a
lawyer. I stayed there about three weeks, and during those three
weeks I realized that everything was the same, that everyone
recognized me and I recognized every corner of the city just as
I had left it. And in three weeks I realized that nothing would
be as it was before, yeah, nothing was ever going to be like
before, nothing, because Monkey Castrejon and the Dog who
had gone to study in Arequipa and who also returned at the
same time, told me that Adriana was going to get married, pal,
yeah, she was marrying the very same boyfriend who she had
cheated on.

"But there are more women in life," the Dog said and
he moved his eyes around to give me some examples but he
couldn't find any because that afternoon only those who had
hung out together in high school got together at Quarter Tango's house, and we roasted a lamb and we were slurping down
the last of the wine from the Velazquez year-end harvest. So
when the Dog snooped around searching for a female, the only
thing he found was a group of idiots turning the grill while the
others said, Cheers, brother.

"Seems as though they are getting married in a hurry," the
Monkey said.

I felt something go Crack! inside of me and I felt that a part
of my past had gone to the inner pit of hell. Because despite
everything, despite the fight that I had in front of her house, despite the fact that she left me for her cuckolded boyfriend, despite all that, I had always held a dream, an illusion of running
into each other at another dance or in another bathroom like

what had happened before, but that illusion had just received a
low blow and it was being shattered even as the Monkey kept
talking, telling me that he didn't want to tell me about it, but
he had to tell me about it, and I, lying, told him that it wasn't
a problem, Monkey, because what I had with her I had gotten
over a long time ago.

And Rudy the Tank showed up with a jug of wine and a
glass in his hand, and without hearing one smidgen of my con-
versation said, Cheers, brother! to those women even though
they treat you mean, and he gave me the jug and a glass. Rudy
the Tank was already loaded to the gills with a breath that would
intoxicate anyone, and he told me this morning that he had seen
his godson, Miss Goalie's kid.

"Have you seen him, Tito? You ought to meet him, brother,
the little kid is quite sharp."

"Surely," and Rudy the Tank talked and talked and I kept
thinking about Adriana who was getting married to her cuckolded boyfriend and with whom she would have a child when
that child should be with me and he should be named Rudy like
you.

"Are you listening to me, brother? Because that kid is so
sharp he doesn't seem to be his parents' kid."

"And drink to that, Tank," and also for her even though
she's paying for it and she's marrying someone else and having
someone else's children."

"And you know that my godson is very intelligent but he
doesn't have any future because the President is splashing
around in the jungle rivers to look to stir up some kind of shit
in the Orinoco."

"Everything is a great tragedy, isn't it? And with the brains
that this kid was born with as a result of the biochemical effect
of screwing with a birth control pill stuck on the end of his
father's dick."

"That's how it is, brother."

"Yeah, it's a complete tragedy that Adriana is getting married to that guy in this ugly soap opera."

"Yeah, ugly."

"And that she end up pregnant and that she forget about our tongues in the bathroom, and what we would name our first-born and what a tragedy without Adriana in the future."

"Exactly," the Tank said, "there is no future."

"What shall we do then, Tank?"

"The answer, Tito, is in your hands." And I looked at the glass of wine that I was holding.

"Tie one on?"

"I agree completely, brother. I have always followed you, Tito, since you were a little kid. And I'm going to continue to follow you in this, so when you least expect it, I'll tie one on."

The three weeks in Tacna flew by. Yes, they flew by, and my mother with her cloud-like smile that traverses the sky had already gone shopping for some pants and shirts that she placed carefully folded at the bottom of my suitcase, and she also put in some socks that I had brought from Lima with holes that looked like mice bites and that she had mended, and she put in some canned jellies, peaches and cherries, and taffy that they only knew how to make in Tacna, at the Berrios' house on the outskirts of the city, out there where there wasn't even any track of asphalt but dirt roads surrounded by sugar cane plantations. And so the suitcase kept getting fatter and fatter and my mother called me to help her, to tell me that she couldn't close it, because between what she had bought for me and what I was taking back it was impossible to close it, and then I sat down on the bed and she was able to close the zipper and tie the straps. Ready! she told me, and here in your handbag I put some cookies and a little fresh fruit for the trip that is quite long, and take this also, and my mother gave me a print of Saint Benito, and carry it with you always and have a lot of faith in him because he is the saint of impossible things.

"And do you believe that my impossibilities can be possible some day?"

"It's a matter of faith, son?"

Then a spark that was a mixture of pride and sadness sprang

from her eyes again, because her son was returning to the capital again, he was going to study to be a lawyer and she was
also hoping to say some day, my son the J.D., like a Uruguayan
author had written it, but as a last resort, as a last resort, her son
was leaving again, and again that spark of pride and sadness
appeared.

Once again in Lima, and of course, once again Julia desir-
ous of renewing her seventeen years with my seventeen years
and I happy in life joining her thirty-four years. That was the
time that I was already visiting her house although her parents would look at us with a long face because Julia's daughter
learned my name among her first words. Afterwards her old
lady began to feel affection towards me. She didn't think Julia
would stay with me for the rest of her life, but she showed affection towards me. Her old man, on the other hand, couldn't
tolerate me for shit, and as far as he was concerned this entire
romance was an act of perversity and degenerate. Me, simply
quiet as could be, acting like a dumbshit, completely...

And the years went by, little by little without realizing it
they went by, and in those years the last Viceroy of Peru didn't
pay attention to the warnings and suggestions of Adriana's father and he let everything continue as if it were a snowball that
kept rolling and rolling because the terrorists had already put
their flag on more than one side. That's how Rudy the Tank already a guerilla agent told me one of the many times I returned
to Tacna and before he involved the old lady of this story with
I'll plant a bomb and then I'll hide (that is, in secrecy), because
that was his choice. I always hoped not to have any influence
on his decision. But I don't know, who knows. Sometimes they
would give me reasons that I didn't grasp. And out there the
evil Tacnean gossipers were saying that they had sent *the Tank*
to the capital and that he was one of those who from time to
time left the city black as coffee armed to the nines, and son
of a bitch, another black out! Where are the candles because
you can't see shit? Because it wasn't just in the hills that things
were getting rough, really rough in fact, it also got really hairy

in Lima, first with the towers a little later with car bombs on a corner least expected, and then later with a general exile that seemed uncontrollable.

"Six guerillas," Mañuco told me one afternoon who was already Lieutenant Mañuco and he didn't whore around in the brothels in Callao but he had his own little whore in a house on Fifth Street who had seduced him and made him faithful to her using her famous pose like Kennedy's death at the blink of an eye. Six terrorists are needed to make a car bomb that will down a bank, a theater, a television station, whatever you want to fly, brother.

The last Viceroy had just left the country, everything in disorder, everything upside down, and his time in government was already over, and his party, not even joking would win again and who would have imagined that the new government would do the impossible, that is, mess up everything even more than it already was. It was election day and I had already decided to nullify my vote because I truly didn't believe in any candidate. I had already decided to do it, so my political conscience was at ease, if such a thing can exist since the first politically unconscious are the politicians. After all, I found myself in such an enormous historical-existential decision when I received a letter that came from Arequipa. The Monkey wrote me and told me that he would vote a blank ticket, and he also told me that last week the Dog had had an attack of immeasurable deepness and he head out walking towards the crater of a volcano in Arequipa and he had decided to crawl into that very same crater, yeah, in the crater, through one of those holes that are found in the volcano hills where the eruptions or burps leak out, yes the Dog wanted to crawl right in there to measure the internal deepness and to find a deep answer to this country full of bombs and economic crises. They stopped him when he was about to reach the top, and they carried him away while he barked rabidly that we had to know the deep Peru. But this is not all the news, the Monkey's letter said, because after Adriana got married and moved to Arequipa, from time to time the

Monkey ran into her with her cuckolded groom at receptions, parties or at the movies, and once he ran into them in the country when the Monkey was knawing on a guinea pig, bone and all and they were searching for a table where they could see the paths of Arequipa. The Monkey gave the guinea pig a break for a second, greeted them, of course, he invited them to his table but they didn't accept, and she looked happy, you know, happy as heck, above all because after losing her child shortly after he was born and she still had all that little sky blue baby clothing, and the cradle made by a carpenter from Sabandia and the rattles and the baby bottle and a little T-shirt with Bolo on it, after all that Adriana experienced a depression that seemed to reflect Adriana's shadow and although the sun in that city was shining itself to exhaustion there wasn't anything that could make her shine. They say that time heals all, and if that's not true, then it ends up killing you. It must have been the cure of time in this case, because the Monkey had seen her in a good mood. She even made fun of the pounds that the Monkey had gained, and he answered that yes he had, that they were a result of his investments in Arequipa beer and he touched his belly that was already starting to hang over his belt. Then Adriana told him that they were leaving Arequipa, and they were leaving Peru because Adolfo had received a scholarship to complete his Masters in the United States, and both of them were going there, they were leaving soon, almost right after the elections. The Monkey couldn't remember the name of the city. It wasn't Miami, or Chicago, or New York or any of those cities that everyone had heard about at least once. It was a city with a very gringo name, but the Monkey promised to find out well. I don't know why. And really, I didn't know why I would want to know where Adriana was going with her cuckolded husband, why know it when I only felt that every day she was farther away, impossibly far away. After all, Arequipa is on the road from Lima to Tacna; the United States wasn't on any of my roads. Then I went to vote for the new President, and I nullified my vote because like Quarter Tango would sing, *today a prom-*

ise, tomorrow a betrayal.

It was a Thursday. Yes, I remember that it was a Thursday several months after the elections that the Aprists won. A tiring Lima Thursday with a sky uniformly gray that didn't let out a wink of sun. I had finished all my classes and I didn't feel a bit like studying anything, so I decided to throw myself belly-up on the bed while I stared at the humidity stains left stamped on the roof. And that's how I was, thinking about twenty years back, when I went into a bathroom, and I stood there totally speechless in front of a five year old girl, thinking that by now she would be in an *American bathroom, perhaps she is taking a shower right now, could you pass me a towel, sweetheart?*, and suddenly Quarter Tango opens the door almost breaking it:

"They caught him!"

"What?"

"They caught Rudy."

They had found him in a small cove room that he had in Surquillo while he was taking a sinister nap on top of an industrial-sized mountain of terrorist flyers that could have wallpapered the national stadium. More proof, impossible.

And then we went to the police station at Surquillo with Mañuco. Only he saw him in the jail cell. Mañuco said he found the Tank squatting in a corner, his face between his knees that he barely raised to be able to recognize him with a look that showed no signs of being clear.

"Oh! It's you."

Mañuco didn't know what to say and he sought refuge in cigarettes as an excuse. The Tank held out an arm. He smoked.

"We're going to get you out of here soon. You'll see, pal, soon."

Two cockroaches ran in between them. He smoked another cigarette.

"Even though Señor de Locumba helps you, I don't think that you'll get me out of here. It's more screwed up than passing the exam to get into high school."

And he smoked again.

"Don't forget the old times. Happen what may, we will always be together."

"I remember more about the present time."

Then it was Mañuco who needed to light a cigarette to defend him. He needed the smoke. He needed the silence.

"It's not about that now, Tank."

"Oh, no? And then what's it about?"

"Getting you out of here."

"Why? Haven't you noticed that we're on opposite sides?" *the Tank* said.

"Yes, I believe so. But anyway, you are still my friend."

"You should have said that before your subordinates tore my soul apart."

"I just found out."

"Oh! The intelligence service is a little slow."

"Fuck you, Tank."

"I'm not the one who's fucking, pal. And honestly, I hope you don't come out asking why I got involved in this if we all came from the same group."

"Tito says he knows the answer to that question. I even believe that he blames himself."

"Yes, Tito. I would have liked to have him close by when they grabbed me."

"And didn't you ever think that I could be out there?" Mañuco said.

"I've thought about it sometimes."

"And what would happen if we ran into each other again not like now, but in another…circumstance?"

"Another circumstance?"

"You know what I am talking about. You and me, Tank, on opposite sides."

"I don't know, pal, I don't know. And you?"

"Me neither."

"Do me a favor, Mañuco: it would be better for you not to get me out of here, to avoid any circumstance."

And the Tank tolerated life by the thread of his life, and after having him for about a month at the Surquillo police station they sent him to a jail on an island where not even a shadow could escape. Visiting him there, don't even mention it, it was almost impossible, and besides he didn't want for anyone to visit him. I found out from his parents that he had a lawyer. A good one according to them. And I didn't hear anything more about the Tank until much later. In these times I also had my changes. Not as drastic as Rudy's, but moves, nevertheless. For some time my old man had fostered the idea of buying a small apartment in Lima.

"It's that money in the bank turns into water, son."

"I know, dad."

"Because there is no interest that can keep up with this inflation."

"I know that also, dad."

"But at least let me put forth my reasoning before you contradict me, okay?"

"I still haven't started to contradict you."

"Then, listen to me, even if it's only this one time."

"I'm telling you that I already have my ears standing up like two satellites."

"Because my idea, son, is to buy a small apartment here in Lima. You're listening to me, right?"

"..."

"You are already going to graduate and since you are studying law, and maybe, I don't know, maybe you are thinking about staying in Lima. I don't know, that is your decision, and you could live in the apartment, of course, and we would have a place to stay whenever we felt like visiting you, and if you prefer to return to Tacna, well, in that case we would rent it out and that's all. What do you think about that proposal, son?"

For the second time in this story I didn't contradict my father. So for several weeks the two of us went around looking at buildings, condominiums and buildings under construction until finally we found an apartment that was quite pleasant right on Arequipa Avenue. I didn't want my dad to put it in my name but the old man insisted and over-insisted until I ended up accepting. The next week I left the boarding house at 820 Leon Velarde, while Mrs. Blanca cried like a Magdalene so much so that she flooded the house and my entire shirt because she was crying while hugging me, and well, I had lived in that boarding house for several years and the lady's affection had grown for me and mine for her also, but now it was time to leave.

I left to live in my apartment, to live somewhat alone, somewhat with Julia who sometimes decided not to return to her house therefore making my nights nightless. Julia had also moved a few months before I had. She didn't put up with her father's last outburst that went back to calling her a whore and all its dressings and he also called her a degenerate because over the last years she had corrupted a snot-nosed kid like me who was no longer so snot-nosed but who was still far too young for her. This time the boo hoo made by Julia's mother was not sufficiently persuasive, and her daughter finished closing the buckles on that suitcase that was older than the arrival of the railroad to Peru she grabbed Maria Lucero by the hand and she left without saying Ciao! at first she stayed in a hotel for a few days, but shortly she rented a small apartment in Barranco, very close to the plaza with the same name. So after I moved, there were nightless nights at her house, and an equal number in mine.

I remember that we were in my apartment eating a breakfast of coffee and scrambled eggs with small pieces of ricotta cheese crumbled into it to recuperate our burnt-up energy, and also, of course, some crusty bread fresh out of the ovens from the bakery on Petit Thours Avenue, when I told Julia that I had received a letter from Dante who was working as a pilot in Montreal and who told me that it was a cold there that we could not imagine, but that the city was heavenly and that he had a Canadian sweetheart, and also that Canada had an open-door policy for immigrants, especially for those who had studied something, whatever, anything from carpentry to a neurologist who specialized in sky-blue colored neurons limping on one foot, in any kind of profession, but in some profession, and of course, in his letter he told me, you should be about finished with law school and you could do a Masters in International Law, and if you want, my house is here for you, brother.

Julia listened to me without saying a word. Surely she thought about it more than twice because that's how she had become, thinker of everything twice over.

"Considering the way things are around here, it wouldn't be a bad idea; besides, even if you go it doesn't mean that you won't return."

I told her that I had told Dante's tale to her just to tell her, and that was the absolute truth because at that time I had no interest in making plans to leave Peru.

"Why don't you ask at the Consulate? After all, what have you got to lose?"

And I ended up at the Consulate speaking to an extremely amicable diplomat, so friendly that I ended up thinking that he wanted something from me, but no, I don't believe so, and he gave me several university addresses where they offered a Masters in International Law, not only in Montreal, but also in Toronto and Calgary, and suddenly he told me that he could begin the paperwork for a visa, why wait, start the paperwork now. So without knowing exactly why nor for what reason, I ended up with a Canadian visa and a list of universities that I never wrote to.

At that time we became tighter financially because of the shortage of money and inflation that was no longer a pot of toasted corn but rather a helium-filled balloon that had no limits on rising. My old man had invested a good amount of his savings in our apartment, but still, and for a rather long time, we had to keep paying for it. Then again Julia, the double-thinker on everything, the seventeen-years-older than me Julia, told me why didn't I rent it and pay for it with the rent.

"Yes, but...in that case I'd have to pack up my bags for 820 Leon Velarde.

And Julia with her seventeen-years-older than me, Julia the

double-thinker, even more, Julia with everything thought out and doubly thought out, told me that she could get me a small place.

"What do you say, Tito? Do you want to move in with me and Maria Lucero?"

If one were to say the same thing to me today, I would do a semiotic and psychoanalytic analysis of the proposition to move before giving a millimeter of a response, but back then I didn't care anything about that, and so I pounced upon her and planted a kiss on her—which was the best way I had of saying yes—and it ended up with both of us in the middle of the breakfast table.

It wasn't difficult to find a renter for the apartment, and after so many candidates, a couple around thirty years of age showed up, a woman with hard tits and no bra, and the guy, well, I don't even remember what he looked like, and the two of them looked at the apartment from top to bottom, they liked it, and we signed the lease. They always paid on time, something rather rare in this country, and I never heard a complaint about them except for a couple of times when the building concierge told me, you know, young man, strange people come to visit your renters, really young man, when it's my turn for night watch I have seen some strange people.

I didn't pay much attention, and they kept paying their rent on time (me picking up the check and copping a look at her hard tits with no bra), and my father's apartment—mine according to him—ended up paying for itself.

"Son of a bitch, the Tank!"

I was reheating some stew when I turned on the television: the one o'clock news, a terrorists' riot at different prisons.

"Son of a bitch!"

And suddenly all the bright images of Rudy the Tank: Rudy on the soccer field who yells at me to pass him the ball, who is alone in front of the goal hoop, and it's coming at you Tank, a goal by damn, a goal Tito, we made a goal and the game is over, we beat the other team by four, Tank, we beat them, Tito.

And Rudy the Tank and me jumping the school walls and escaping by running at full speed into the middle of the street, our sweaters flying like flags, to hell with school today. And Rudy the Tank drinking rum along Bolognesi Boulevard and drunk until he got tired, *salud*, brother, to women even if they treat you badly. And Rudy the Tank in the hospital after fainting on the road to the church of Señor de Locumba, promises are promises, right, Tank?

"...the marines from the war attacked one of the prisons," the TV anchor was saying.

And like intermittent lights, the images of the Tank became entangled, they superimpose themselves and reappear innumerable times in my memory until I begin to intuit that he begins to be that: an act of my memory.

The story does not stop there: Ortega, Ortega son as he was known to us, the one who wore his straight-legged pants up to his chest, Captain Ortega many years later, the captain who received the order to attack the prison, ended up flat on his back on the island with a bullet in his chest. So on the next day, everyone, at least almost all of us who lived in Lima, went from wake to wake. First we had an early morning mass for Ortega son and there was Ortega father torn to pieces, of course, and this time he recognized me, he recognized all of us, he forgot about those years that my father flattened him with a single smack, and then he hugged Mañuco, my condolences, sir, he hugged Quarter Tango, I hugged him, and he struggled to speak, my son's friends.

From there, of course, to Rudy's funeral, because you couldn't get out of going to the mass, the Tank, although during your final days you would have proclaimed that religion was the people's opium, and even if you were to resurrect revolutionarily to snuff out the church where we were keeping vigil over you. Your parents, surely you saw them from your second-rate casket, went to pieces and your mother's soul ripped apart as well as anyone's eardrums who heard her weeping. We hugged them too, you know, you checked on us, we also felt that they recognized us as my son's friends, and we stayed for quite a while, and during that time your old man told me that the soldiers didn't give you a chance to defend yourself. And your old man's voice was cracking, Tank, because I know my son wasn't a saint, no, no he wasn't a saint by any means. Your old man knew you well, Tank. Because a father is a father when he knows what his son is involved in. And our old man's voice broke up again, Tank. And what do I say back to him? Give me a clue, Tank. Come out of your casket and prompt me on how I have to calm him down. Tell him what... tell him... look, sir, it pisses me off as much as it does you that the Tank has died. Honestly, sir, because he and I were like that: like a hand in a glove. He was the hand I was the glove. And it's screwed up, sir, to be a glove without a hand. And you know what is even more screwed up, sir? You are not going to believe me, but the Tank was faithful as hell. Honestly, he always listened to me, he never failed me. He even wanted to beat up the cheating girl's boyfriend the first time Adriana deceived me. And what really sucks right now, sir, is that I didn't listen to the Tank when he would go off on his enlightening matters. No, I didn't listen to him because that afternoon I found out that Adriana was getting married and I tied one on so bad that I ended up retching until I had dry heaves. Don't get mad, sir, but that's how it was. And don't get mad either because I went to the police station where they first took the Tank. I was there, sir, with Quarter Tango and with Mañuco. Of course I was there. And Mañuco told him I'll get you out of here, brother. Those were his exact words, sir. The Tank himself is a witness. But he didn't accept. And when I tried to see him in his cell the Tank himself told me not to come in. It was the first time he didn't pay attention to me. He had freed himself from me. You freed yourself from me, Tank. Shall I tell your old man that? Should I tell him that I should have shit on your independence so that I would have made myself listen like one ought to? Yes, I should have told you, don't give me that negative crap because I'm not going to leave you in this police station or in any other. But I didn't say anything.

And that's why, that's why I feel that I have failed you, Tank. I failed you when you were loyal as hell to me. That's fucked up, and I would like to know, brother, what I could do to deserve your forgiveness. Yes, give me a clue, Tank, get out of your second-hand casket and whisper in my ear what I have to do. And this time I promise not to fail you. Sincerely, brother. And I'll keep waiting, Tank, for you to tell me something, and if you can't tell me anything like I'm talking to you, at least tell it to me through my dreams.

And Mañuco, Quarter Tango and I ended up that evening— night was already starting—at Miss Blanca's. There, in her little dining room. The three of us seated. And wall-to-wall silence. Miss Blanca left a thermos of hot water, coffee and sugar, some bread in case we wanted to make snacks. But we did nothing. Until Mañuco made himself a coffee, and he pulled out a flask of rum that was stuck in his pants and poured rum into his coffee. Evening disappeared, the memory remained. No one spoke. Not about the Tank, not about Ortega son. Nothing moved either. Only Mañuco: his third coffee, rum in the coffee, when I asked him if he felt like getting drunk. Nothing but silence from his face, although you could see that the words were imprisoned in his stomach. Then he threw down an unending swallow from the mouth of the bottle and he looked at us with fearful eyes. He wanted to talk. And he hesitated. He trembled. He searched for support: his hand grasping the bottle.

"You don't know," he told us, looking at us, and then immediately hiding his look in some faded flowers on the plastic tablecloth.

"You don't know," he repeated, raising his eyes towards us, "but I was there, with Ortega son."

He told us that they had sent the two of them to the rearguard, and they saw everything from the embarkation point, the prison torn to shreds as if it were a war, and the few terrorists that were still alive were face down. As they were arriving with their soldiers, everything was already, or almost already, under control.

"It's turned into shit, brother."

Then Ortega son gave orders to disembark and Mañuco stayed behind, only a little behind.

"He was waiting until his people arrived on the island," Mañuco said.

And that was the moment when he saw him walk so confidently, so on the moon, or maybe, so trapped by the fear of smoke that he got lost and confused by the clouds, and in a split second Mañuco remembered those years in school when Quarter Tango carried his porno magazines and Ortega son without knowing what to do, with innocence in his eyes, and without knowing what to do.

"And I shouted at him with all my soul."

Stop trusting life, Ortega son, because these weren't those school days and Professor Grover nor the priest were there to protect him, Ortega son, hide your chest, your face, because one never knows about the terrorists, because it didn't matter if he wasn't a hero, we all preferred for him to be alive, even if he had to hide, everyone, including his old man, Ortega son. But Mañuco's voice didn't even reach the shore.

"I myself saw his legs bending."

Falling with his chest forward towards the clouds, looking, already almost sightless.

"I ran to where he was, but there wasn't anything left to do."

Then Ortega son showed a shadow of a smile and with innocence in his eyes he seemed to ask Mañuco about a bullet that wasn't written about in any navigation manual.

"And he finished screwing me with that look."

Mañuco wasn't sure about the rest.

"I know that I fired several times."

He didn't know where. If it was in the air, at the prisoners that were spread out, or at the sand. He only knew that in an instant his own soldiers unarmed him.

"He's wasted several terrorists, my lieutenant," they told him.

He was no longer firing but it as if he still had the taste of blood in his mouth. Then shortly he approached the truck where they were carrying the cadavers.

"Maybe they're loading more than one of the ones that you downed," one soldier told him.

And he stood there paralyzed.

"What's wrong, my lieutenant?"

He recognized you, yes, Mañuco had seen him. He said he came closer, he doubted for a second that he wanted to believe that he was mistaken, that he touched your forehead...

"What's wrong, lieutenant, sir?"

...that he embraced you with all his strength.

INDIGO BLUE SKY

* * *

After Mañuco's tremendous confession, glasses, chairs, the thermoses of hot water began to fly and in the middle of all that mess they slugged him time and again and he didn't even defend himself, because in the theory of the mirror which you, Mañuco, had invented, in that theory in which we were the same figure but reversed, in that theory you never spoke about crushing the body and soul of one of our own.

And afterwards days of a monolithic silence overcame me.

"What's wrong with you?" Julia would say to me.

I don't know, but I couldn't bring myself to tell her anything. I read all the newspapers. Page by page, article by article, and that's how I found out that they would punish the military heads that had destroyed the prisons, and I also found out that they didn't talk about or name Mañuco. And Julia was already bordering on being fed up with my answers that weren't answers while Maria Lucero grew frightened, extremely frightened. One could see it in her little eyes. You could see it when she found me buried in a stack of newspapers or almost hypnotized by the eight o'clock news that reported a new coup against terrorism.

But that night Julia was giving me a hard time, telling me that I couldn't go on like that, I can't live with you like you are nor can Maria Lucero when suddenly the telephone rang and I answered it to escape her reproaches.

"Hello, young man!" It was the doorman who guarded the building where I rented the apartment.

"Hey, man," and his voice sounded full of fright as if someone was watching him.

"What's wrong?" I asked.

And Julia forgot about the shouting and not being able to live like that and her eyes widened intuiting some unexpected news.

"What's wrong?" I repeated and on the other end there was an instance of silence.

"They've taken away your renters."

"What?"

"You remember that I told you those people were strange, that they always got together at night. You remember that I told you that? Well right now they just took them off. They took both of them off for being terrorists."

"Son of a bitch."

"And not only that, young man. The police also asked me who the owner of the apartment was. And I gave them your name. What was I to do, I had to give your name. And they asked me for your address and I told them that I didn't know where you were living, and that's the truth because all I have is your telephone number. But in my opinion they think that you are involved with terrorists, young man."

I didn't know whether to thank him or what, but he hung up immediately and for an infinite instant the only sound to be heard was the sharp shrill of the telephone dial tone until Julia asked what had happened.

"Nothing, Julia, nothing."

"What do you mean, nothing?"

"They screwed me, but nothing's wrong."

Thus began the story of a Peruvian under pursuit whose only interest in life had been to fuck his brains out with an ex-aerobics teacher and secretly remembering a girl that he met in a bathroom. Of course, the Peruvian in the last part of this story was more scarred than a thorn-scratched record. Especially since Lieutenant Mañuco said who knows, but who knows what, perhaps Mañuco himself was the one who had shot *the Tank* in the back. And the Peruvian didn't tell anyone that the whole thing screwed him up and he didn't know what the hell to do to bring the Tank back to life and turn things backwards, far backwards in this story to that afternoon in Tacna eating grilled meat with no talk of bombs, friend, you have to be self-controlled, and pay attention to me and not to your damn terrorists. But he didn't tell anyone. Not to the ex-aerobics teacher, nor to his parents, not even to his own shadow. And then he got the idea to go even further back in this story. There, to a scene with Adriana. A scene that happens at the door of her house. The door, flowers and grass all around. Adriana is waiting at the door. He enters. He looks at her. No, no, that's not how he looks at her. Not with those horny eyes that are more appropriate for Julia than for a fifteen-year old Adriana. The scene repeats itself. Now that's it. With that look. A stupid little look, but with that look. And they speak. I don't know exactly what they say, but they say something. And in that scene the Peruvian finds the Tank's resurrection. Yes, he feels a sense of relief in his soul when he thinks about telling the whole mess to Adriana, and she tells him (or she tells me, and this part I do remember well because all of this was a dream): I understand you, Tito, because I always understood you, I didn't want to tell you although I always knew what was going to happen to Rudy, that's why I agreed to name our child after him, because our child will always pay attention to you regardless of what you tell him. Don't you remember that we talked about that? Let's have a child, let's name him Rudy. What do you think? It would even be a way of bringing him back to life, wouldn't it? And it was precisely then that I woke up, exactly when that revelation came to me and where Adriana might be, where, where, in which state in the United States, but I have to see her and tell her everything, and suddenly a quarrel with Julia, and the telephone, hey, young man.

"What do you mean nothing's wrong?" the ex-aerobics teacher said in the middle of a neurotic dance.

And so continued the story of this Peruvian under pursuit by his compatriots because that very night I disappeared from the apartment and hid out around Callao, in Pocho's boarding house. Three nights later I was at Jorge Chavez airport taking a plane to Canada. Quarter Tango and Julia had bribed the immigration officer.

"He's a fat man with a handle-bar mustache. Don't get in

any other line because he's the one who will know you," Quarter Tango said.

"But I don't want to go to Canada."

"Then what do you want?"

"I would like to have a child with Adriana, and give him a name that I'm thinking about."

"Fuck you, Tito."

"You asked me what I wanted."

"You know that the police already went to your apartment to look for you.

"Yeah, Julia told me." Luckily, nothing had happened to Julia and her daughter.

"So it would be better for you to forget about Adriana for a while."

"I can't."

"Julia is paying for your ticket to Canada, the bribe to immigration and you keep on thinking about Adriana."

"It's because I can't stop thinking about her."

"What kind of shit are you talking about?"

"About a dream."

"Stop dreaming because reality is fucked up."

"Okay, okay. Can I ask for one more favor?"

"Yes, of course."

"Tell my parents goodbye for me. Julia said not to call them because surely they have tapped their phone."

"Don't worry. I'm going to Tacna next week and I'll talk with them."

"Quarter Tango…"

"What?"

"Thanks, brother-in-law."

Fat man with a handle-bar mustache. It must be that one because he looked like the type who accepted bribes.

"Passport?"

He opened it to the first page. He typed my name into the computer. Julia and Quarter Tango were standing behind. I was almost peeing in my pants from fear and I think I'll tell Adriana that too when I see her. The fat man looked at the information in the computer. He looked at me. He recognized me. Yeah, fat cheeks with an Emiliano Zapata mustache, it's me, you let yourself be bought out for me, fat cheeks, and surely you think that I killed someone, isn't that right, fat cheeks? He typed something into the computer. He typed again. His fat cheeks swelled up. I was double pissing now, in indicative and subjunctive, maybe the fat man won't let me go through. He types in again.

"Everything is in order, have a nice trip."

I didn't say anything. Not even a thank you, fat cheeks. I looked back: Quarter Tango and Julia breathing again, smiling again, waving goodbye with their hands. And suddenly Julia crying. I made a gesture to go back towards where they were, but Julia signaled "no" with her head, a sign of "go ahead" with her arm, and for the first time I saw that in the last few nights her forty-some years had suddenly landed on her and without even asking for permission. And she kept on crying because she knew that that trip didn't carry a return date, and she also knew, of course she knew, that she would stay there and almost with no alternative ever, to return again to those seventeen years.

"I already know the whole mess. Julia called me and told me what happened. So you have become a political refugee," Dante said.

"Really, not long ago I became the pursuer so that they would stop pursuing me."

"And what the hell are you pursuing?"

"A woman whose name begins with "A", ends with "A", and has another "A" in the middle."

"Oh!"

"Do you know someone?"

"I know Triple AAA, but it deals with cars, not with women."

And Dante took me to his house. My potential Masters in International Law came to a screeching halt because I never got to graduate as a lawyer in Lima. But I enrolled in an Institute for Foreigners to learn French that at the beginning I understood by accident because it was a romance language and later I began to chew it with a heavy Peruvian accent. I also had a tourist visa not a work permit, which expired shortly and that's when my years of being illegal began. What I wouldn't have done at that time for a few dollars. Waiter, receptionist in a hotel for quickies, I painted entire houses, I laid wall to wall carpet in apartments, I tutored private Spanish classes, I was a lifeguard at YMCA pools, I banged some old ladies who were more wrinkled than I don't know what, I did anything for a few bucks, except screwing men, just in case.

At first when I left Peru, Julia and I called each other by phone almost weekly. Really, she called; truthfully. I kept thinking about my dream of Adriana. Later, the phone calls were not quite as frequent. Later we agreed to stop the phone calls—the bill was getting too high—and we promised to write to each other about everything that was happening in our lives. But the letters came farther and farther apart and one day winter came and there were no more letters from Julia. I didn't know whether to be happy or sad: maybe she had met someone seventeen years older than me, maybe there was no longer a motive to wait for my return without a return date maybe that was better.

I lived with Dante for quite some time until I got a horny turn-on for a stripper who I met in downtown Montreal.

"What's your name?" I asked her.

She was dancing on a small runway in front of me. In a flash and at an inch and a half from my eyes nose mouth she flipped off the tanga that covered her (if one can use the word cover in this case) and I confirmed that her tan was complete, extremely complete, and I also proved that the serenity of her nakedness unleashed any control over my intimate parts hidden under my clothing.

"My name is Norma," she said in perfect French.

"I believe that all norms are made to be broken," I said in perfect Spanish, keeping the play on her name.

"*¿Hablas español?*" she said. "My mother is from Madrid and I understand everything."

"Then you agree."

"With what?"

"That all rules are made to be broken."

"That depends," she said.

"Does it depend on the violator?"

"And also on the rule, right?"

That's how we met and that night we slept together. At first she refused to go out with me because her rule was not to get involved with clients. But I convinced her, telling her that the exception makes the rule, Norma. We had sex for a thousand and one nights, and in a thousand and one places including the snows of Montreal. The Peruvian under pursuit or the pursuer of a woman whose name has three "A"s in it, seemed to have abandoned his search until after the thousand and one nights a letter arrived from Arequipa.

"Who is writing to you, Tito?" she said from the bed.

"My friend the Monkey."

The Peruvian under pursuit opened the letter. He kept reading. He read more. He finished the letter and Norma pulled him into bed with an octopus arm.

"What's wrong?"

"Nothing."

"And what's wrong with that guy down here?"

"He's on strike from exhaustion."

"Okay, it's better to leave him alone until tonight."

The one thousand and second night was equally deceiving for Norma. The Peruvian under pursuit kept thinking about the letter in which Monkey Castrejon gave him Adriana's address. "I'm fulfilling my promise late"—the Monkey wrote—"but here's her address." She lived in a city called Pittsburgh, and the Peruvian under pursuit had looked on a map about twenty times that day to see where Pittsburgh is and he had already found out how you get to that city with such a strange name. "Furthermore, a little gossip"—the Monkey wrote in a P.S.— "in Tacna they told me that Adriana is about to break up with her cuckolded groom-husband."

On the thousand and third day the Peruvian under pursuit avoided another deception with Norma when she wrapped another octopus arm around him.

"I'm going to the United States," I told her.

"But you don't have a visa to get in."

"It doesn't matter."

"If they catch you they'll deport you to Peru where they think you are a terrorist."

"It doesn't matter. I'm going even if all the tides are against me, including you."

"And what are you going to do in the United States?"

"Let's say that I am going to search for a woman who I met in a bathroom to have a child with her. Does that sound logical?"

She sat there thinking.

"It sounds more logical for us to ball before you leave."

"I can't."

"Well, it's a matter of logic. There's no saying goodbye without a good screw."

"I can't. You've already proven it. There's no reaction."

"I can help you, Tito," and she wiped her tongue across her upper lip.

"That's not it. I have to save up my sex resources for the woman I'm going to have a child with."

"You are a hopeless nut."

"That's where I'm headed: let's see if they can fix me."

And the pursued-pursuer Peruvian left. I left Montreal on a bus (Dante stood there waving his hand at the station and surely that night he cleaned the house four times from pure nervousness that he had acquired from my departure) and I arrived at the last bus stop in the south, Cornwall. From there I took a taxi and I told the driver to take me to the closest point of the border that he could get me but the farthest from immigration control. The guy got a strange look on his face. He started the motor with his strange face and in less than half an hour he told me, this is it. His face became even stranger when he saw me get out with my bag (it was the only thing that I was carrying) in the

middle of nowhere, or better said, in the middle of the summer
grass. The taxi took off and I looked forward: it was an endless
green. I knew that the Canadian-United States border was not
the hellish battle like that with Mexico, but I also didn't know
very well what it was like. I looked at the endless green again,
I touched the letter with Adriana's address that I was carrying
in my shirt pocket, and the Peruvian under pursuit struck out.
One, two, three miles in the green that seemed endless. And it
remained equally endless until suddenly, as if it had fallen from
the sky, a small horse-driven carriage appeared. The Peruvian
under pursuit thought that the sky and the walk were making
him see things. Don't let it be Rudy's ghost that was driving
the carriage in the middle of this solitude. He rubbed his eyes
a couple of times: the carriage was coming towards him and it
stopped at about three yards from his feet. He saw a man and
a woman—both of them around thirty—dressed completely in
dark clothes.

"What planet did you two fall from?"

"Excuse me, sir."

It was summer with a scorching sun, but the man was
dressed entirely in black with a shirt that was buttoned up to
the neck, a hat with flat flaps, long pants, and he had a pointed
beard that looked as though he had never shaved in his life. The
woman, also entirely in black, wore a long dress down to her
ankles with sleeves that came down to her wrists and it was her-
metically sealed around her neck. Her head was covered with
a bonnet—black, of course—like those that Little Red Riding
Hood used to wear and which didn't allow for you to see even
one hair of her head. So the only skin that was visible were her
hands and her face that displayed two plump cheeks reddened
by the sun that could transform her into the future Queen of the
Apple Festival. The man looked at me with kind eyes:

"Where are you going, sir?"

"To Canton, in the north of New York."

"Then get in."

And I made myself comfortable in the back seat and I fell

asleep from exhaustion. A little while later I found out that they were Amish, a group that lived on the edge of modernity: they didn't use cars, they didn't have televisions nor electricity, it didn't matter to them that Alexander Graham Bell had invented the telephone, and who knows, it didn't occur to me to interview them at the time, to ask them if they used condoms during sex during this period of AIDS. And later I found out that during the middle of my snoring and in a horse-drawn carriage I crossed the border into the United States.

When the man awoke me, we were already in Canton. I thanked them a thousand times over and they disappeared at the corner of a street.

The following morning I left and began to cross all of the northern part of New York State. The scenery was still pastoral at that time of year. But after a few hours on the road the greenness became tiring since the bus stopped in any little town that had three houses in it, twelve people and a couple of dogs. In a city called Harrisburgh, or something like that, I changed buses. Almost all of the seats were taken—I was the last one to get on—and I sat next to an old gringo who had obviously not bathed in a week and who spoke to me in an incomprehensible English without moving his lips where I only answered back to him in a miraculous phrase: Oh, yeah! The bus was a basic brothel: everyone was shouting at everyone else, and a bottle of booze was being passed from hand to hand all the way to the back seats. Before taking off the bus driver asked for silence, and a black man yelled back at him, shut the shit up and drive! Luckily the force of the night took control and without anyone realizing it silence began to reign.

I arrived in Pittsburgh in the morning and I stood there for a minute standing with my bag at the door of the Greyhound station, in the very heart of the city, feeling the five a.m. humidity and the exhaustion that had built up over the course of the entire trip. I pulled out the letter with the address from my pocket and I headed for a taxi:

"To 640 College Street."

"That's in Shadyside, isn't it?" the driver asked.

"Oh, yeah!"

I didn't have the slightest idea and I got in the car and felt that I was just minutes away from reuniting with Adriana, reuniting with her after so many years, rediscovering her three-finger tongue that who knows how much it would measure now.

"640 College. Here it is," the taxi driver said.

An old brick house that they had remade into a building of who knows how many apartments spread out on three floors. 640 College, and I paid and I drew close and looked at the names on the intercom and Adriana with her tongue in its new dimensions would be a doorbell ring away. 640 College, apartment 3. Her name was written there, on the intercom. Adriana's name written by Adriana. Adriana's handwriting after a waterfall of years. 640 College, apartment 3. And my finger glued to the doorbell shouting I want to see Adriana now and forever. Would she still walk towards me like a Greek goddess who escaped from a movie screen? and I want to see Adriana because I have risked my neck crossing the border into this country, hitching a ride like a crazy person in an Amish carriage, forgetting that if they deported me to Peru the police would be proud to destroy another Peruvian's life and they would be happy. I want to see Adriana and my finger fastened to the doorbell until the door made an unpleasant creaking sound and opened up halfway as though saying come forward. On the sides, apartment 1 and apartment 2. Further ahead there was a staircase covered in a tan carpet that led me to the second floor. And there, apartment 3. Doorbell again. Someone walking towards the door. Adriana only seven steps away. Now five. Maybe three. Her hand opening the peephole. The door opens. The door is opening.

"Adolfo, how are you?"

He stood there shocked for an endless instant without knowing what to say, what to do, until he told me, come in, you look tired. He offered me a beer. I took it. Adriana was not there, nor would she be there.

"We are getting divorced," Adolfo confessed to me and I guessed that it was not his decision.

"She left here a month ago already. I know she's still in Pittsburgh but she doesn't want to give me her address."

I took a swallow. I sunk down a little bit in the seat, and I saw that Adolfo did the same.

"Look, Tito, if you want to look for Adriana, that's your business. But if you find her, I promise not to punch you this time."

I smiled before taking another swallow.

"How long have you lived in Pittsburgh?" Adolfo asked me who just minutes before had stopped being the boyfriend-husband of the cheating woman to change himself into a nice guy, although I had the impression, almost with certainty, that in Gringoland he had been cheated on even more.

"I don't live here. I just arrived from Montreal this morning but I don't plan on going back there."

His eyes widened, if you want you can stay here for a few days, although I believe a Peruvian friend of mine is renting some rooms in his house at a good price, are you interested? yes, of course.

And Adolfo picked up the phone, dialed, Hello, Huguito! What's up, brother? Huguito Zegarra was about forty-five years old and had been in Pittsburgh for at least ten years. He came on a Fulbright scholarship to work on a Masters in Political Science, and afterwards he stayed on as a doctoral student in the Education program. Between his Masters and Doctorate his wife Amparo came along with his two daughters, and shortly afterwards they bought a house in Oakland, the neighborhood where the university was. Huguito had built two rooms on the roof of the house that had separate entrances via a spiral staircase that lined the side of the house. You could see the old Oakland neighborhood from one of the rooms and further off, much further off, a building in the form of a medieval cathedral that belonged to the university. From the other side you could see the house's plentiful yard, and at the end, the chocolate-colored

water of one of the rivers that runs through Pittsburgh. I got the
room where you could see the yard and the chocolate-colored
water. There was a girl from Chile living in the other room
who was studying for a Masters in Applied Linguistics (something that I never understood). Her name was Ely and she kept
her room so clean that she made me embarrassed about mine.
For quite a while—the time that the money I had brought from
Montreal lasted—Huguito and I (sometimes Adolfo also) fre-
quented the Latin blasts on weekends, with lots of Budweiser
beer that gave you a beer gut but didn't come close to getting
you drunk, always under the irresistible imperialism of salsa
music. And there, in those binges, I took advantage of asking
about Adriana. Everyone knew her.

"Great chick, Adriana."

"Yeah, she liked to come to parties but I haven't seen her
much lately."

"And she's a great conversationalist, isn't she?"

How many fingers could her tongue have grown, I
thought.

"But you know what, I don't know her address, nor her
telephone number. The one who probably knows is Carolina
because they always used to go swimming together. Come
here, Carol, let me introduce you to Tito, Adriana's friend. Hey
Carol, do you still go to the pool with Adriana?"

"It's been a while since she's gone swimming. Where did
you meet Adriana?"

"In a bathroom."

"Oh, yeah?"

"And Carol, do you know who might have an idea about
Adriana's address?"

"Maybe Marielos. She's the curly-headed girl who is over
there twisting in full swing to the salsa. She should know
because she's the oral newspaper on Latinos in Pittsburgh.
Hey, Marielos, take a little break over here with us after that
dance."

And there was Marielos with her disarrayed ringlets and

saying that she needed to rest because Enrique thinks that dancing is cheating on your partner, and nice to meet you, I'm Marielos.

"This is Tito, he's Peruvian, and Adrianita's friend and he
wants to know where she is."

"That's difficult because your friend has a short-circuited
brain that no one can stop and it's been centuries since I've seen
her. The one I see now is Adolfo, her husband, or ex-husband,
or something like that, who's hot as shit, that son-of-a-bitch.
Don't you like Adolfo, Carol? What you wouldn't do with him
in a couple of nights? Chubby little pervert, you wear your hy-
pocrisy on the outside only. And with the little time that you
have left to finish your studies in medicine. But that crazy Adriana says she's already gotten tired of her husband. That's it,
because now she wants variety. As if that were a new story!
Who doesn't get tired of her husband, who doesn't want a little
variety? And I told that crazy Adriana to have a little fling on
the side, or if she liked, bed a hunk completely but don't let go
of Adolfo. After all, when he is in the midst of an operation during surgery, Adriana can be in full operation banging her fling
on the side and her absolute hunk. But no, that crazy Adriana
didn't pay any attention to me and who knows where she is
now getting it on with her fling. You, Peruvian, do you dance
meringue? Shall we dance the hell out of this meringue?"

"What's wrong, slim?"

"Nothing, Huguito."

"You're a little depressed, aren't you?"

"It must be the winter."

"You still haven't found your little woman who cleans bathrooms."

"There's not a shadow of her. And to top things off, I'm
running short on money, friend, and maybe this month I won't
be able to pay you rent."

Huguito touched his mustache that he dyed black every
Sunday: don't worry, brother, everything has a solution in this
house, but answer me honestly. Do you have AIDS, tuberculo-

sis or syphilis?

"Of course not, Hugo."

"And would it bother you, brother, to stop smoking for a month to earn a few dollars?"

"Of course not."

"Then come with me, slim, because I'm going to show you where the greenback treasures are in this city."

We left the house and took the bus to Fifth Avenue. Huguito was overly mysterious.

"They'll pay you 900 dollars a whack, or better said, for a weekend."

"But what do you have to do, friend?"

"It's very simple, brother. That's it, there they treat you caringly, they feed you well, they give you a good bed, impeccable sheets, they bring you breakfast, but you have to be ready when they call you during the weekend."

There is something fishy here, I told myself. Who pays 900 dollars for a weekend of work? There was an explanation for why Huguito showed up occasionally with super elegant clothes and never said where he had bought them. A bargain, brother, a bargain, was the only thing that he answered. Nine hundred dollars for a weekend: that was hustling Latin lovers.

"I don't know, Huguito. I'm not sure if I can do this shit. Before I did it in Canada, but now I have come for Adriana, and one has his principles."

Huguito told me that everyone in Pittsburgh already knew the story of the skinny little girl in the bathroom because during every drunken stupor I repeated the same thing and ended up singing pathetically Adriana, Adriana, where are you sweetheart.

"But this matter, slim, doesn't deal with principles. It deals with 900 dollars in two days. In two days they stick you a couple of times and you fill your pockets."

"It's that, Huguito, this is the problem. I'm at a stage in my life where I don't want to take any pricks for a few bills."

"What's wrong, slim? Or is it because you faint?"

"No, no, I am very resistant: if you knew about the thousand and one horny nights that I spent with Norma. Or all the bangings one after another that I laid on the old ladies of Montreal."

"That's good. A man with stamina. Let's go down here because we're already close to the laboratory."

Yes, it was a laboratory and with a huge sign half a block long and I didn't know if I should ask Huguito's forgiveness or to ask him why the hell have you brought me here because I don't have rat written on my face. It was a lab and the joke is that they tested medicines on people that had already been tested on monkeys and other similar animals. And of course, they drew your blood every five hours. I didn't stay this time, but I went back. And Huguito was right: they treated me kindly.

"The government has granted an amnesty, son."

"For me, too?"

"Of course for you too. That's why your mother and I have been calling you by phone. Where have you been that we can never find you?"

"I've been letting them suck out my blood."

"Doing what?"

"Nothing, dad, nothing."

"Well, now you can return to Peru."

"Return to Peru? Can I trust that amnesty?"

"Why do you think that I'm calling you long distance?"

"It's just that the politicians lie so much. Besides, I can't go yet, dad."

"Stop screwing with me by contradicting me."

"It's because I still haven't found her, and I can't return without seeing her."

"Seeing her?"

"Yes, I have to see her."

"Who the hell do you have to see?"

"The woman of my future son."

"Oh! Are you drunk? Or have you started taking drugs up there with the Gringos?"

"Let's say that I am searching for a dream that I had."

"And do you know when the hell you are going to wake up so you can return to Tacna?"

Quarter Tango had already taken the fifth taste test of the *picante de mondongo* that was cooking in a copper pot, and a sixth test with a wooden spoon, of course. It's going to be better than shit, brother, because we put in some enticing veal broth and first-rate beef jerky and a hoof, of course, some potatoes and more potatoes so there would be plenty and a shitload of red pepper. I've become an expert on spicy food, brother, Quarter Tango said as the demijohn of red wine from the Velasquez farm remained waiting in a small corner. We were in a large open area, a fourth a mile to the south of Tacna exactly where the infinity of the desert begins, and on that same small piece of land where Quarter Tango had his used car business and from there you could see motors with their bellies opened waiting for pistons, valves, the new crankshaft that still hadn't arrived from the Ordonez workshop, and in that same open space we had found enough room to light a wood fire surrounded and protected by some sun-dried bricks where we put the copper pot. The sun above had reached its hottest peak like a little oven which witnessed this hell of a spicy food that was turning out damn good and the seventh tasting with the wooden spoon, and in Pittsburgh, brother, do people eat their spicy food or at least a little *ceviche*? No, brother, there they fill their bellies with hamburgers and French fries drowning in Ketchup. Poor guys, and an eighth taste, and how can they be a developed country without *picante de mondongo* and without *ceviche*?

In all, I had landed on native soil a few days back because everyone returns and Quarter Tango added: especially when your brow has begun to wrinkle. A lightening trip, exactly thirty minutes in the Miami airport, and a couple of hours in Lima. And from the air, almost upon arriving at Tacna, recognizing those arid hills. Landing and the plane shaking as it touches land. I was on the stairwell. A dark bag over my left shoulder. My parents waiting behind the airport windows. I already saw them. They already saw me, and my mother who waves her arm in a sign of welcome. I already saw them. I already see them and the descending staircase, entrance into the airport, and a hug, that's my son, damn, and my mother saying that I am thin. I tell her it must be because I left half of my blood in Pittsburgh. And my old man philosophically stating that with a couple of red wines the blood would return to my body and soul. And to the house. Then we sat down at the table, my mother had prepared a lamb's tail stew and she tells me that Quarter Tango is going to prepare *picante de mondongo* this weekend. My father cuts off a slice of ricotta cheese the color of fire, and do you want some? It burns like the devil himself, and a little wine to put out the fire, and another, and to your health, and my mother who asks for a glass. Only a little bit of wine, she says, not more than a finger's worth because the wine made by the Velasquez family has always seemed too dry for her. Your mother has never understood wines. But serve me a little anyway, serve me a little because this time I want to toast because it is good, son, to have you back here and a breeze slides through the window, making the curtains dance, and reaching us.

The next day and after a breakfast of *marraquetas* and mountain cheese and fresh milk that still tasted of utter, Quarter Tango arrived in a Hyundai pickup truck and told me that it was already time for me to go because all our friends were asking when you were going to stop traveling and land back here.

"Well, here I am."

And we head out towards the south in the Hyundai, towards the outskirts of Tacna exactly where the desert begins and where Quarter Tango had the cars that he imported, rebuilt and sold. That's how the preparation of this hell of a *picante de mondongo* began while I asked if he knew anything about Julia, and Quarter Tango telling me that I should drop in on Lima, because Julia always remembered me and he was more than sure that I had left a mark on her after everything that had happened. And we started lighting the fire, stacking the small oven with bricks, hanging the copper pot, and Maria Lucero is big, friend, in a few years she'll already start at the university. Soon their friends would come, Quarter Tango said. The Dog also came back from Venezuela where he was working as an engineer, and now he's making hotels with deep foundations throughout all of Tacna, and of course, he came with his Venezuelan wife and their puppy that is exactly like him. Then a taste of this *picante de mondongo* and it has already started to thicken, and the demijohn of red wine is still in the corner because we are waiting for our friends to arrive, and Miss Goalie, stupid as ever, but after all, everything can be found in God's vineyard, and Pocho turned out to be a poet, brother, he received a hell of an award for his poetry and the Monkey is still in Arequipa but he was traveling here last night because he knew that you were going to come and that today we would eat *picante de mondongo* so a little bit longer and he should be showing up here with his beer gut and all because now he looks like a gorilla. And suddenly at the entrance to the open spot Mañuco's face appeared and Quarter Tango telling me that they had worked together since Mañuco left the Navy and returned to Tacna.

"A damn long time, right, friend?" Mañuco says.

"Yes, damn it, too long, since that night that we pummeled you at 820 Leon Velarde because he confessed to us that rage had taken hold of him as if he were a leaf in the wind. A damn long time. Too long. But caring is stronger. It is stronger than the soldier on duty, stronger than terrorists' bombs, stronger than the last recession from the last president. It's stronger and a hug for peace without the peace pipe.

"God damn!" Quarter Tango says.

And the ninth tasting. Maybe the tenth. With the wooden spoon that is. This is already done, friends. I'll give you a hand with the wine, Mañuco says as he heads towards the demijohn of red wine, he uncorks it, he throws it over his right shoulder and from there he starts filling a glass pitcher. Look whose there: at the entrance of the open area, the Monkey, Pocho, the Dog, Miss Goalie, like in the old days, but much older, and a glass of wine, to your health, brother, and the last taste of this hell of a spicy tripe because our friends are here.

And I wake up. I don't know where I am. And little by little I come to realize that this spicy tripe in a copper pot is thousands of miles away.

"Huguito!" I said, entering the kitchen.

"What a face, slim. It looks as though you had seen a ghost."

"More or less. Although I would say it's more like several ghosts in the middle of a pot of *picante de mondongo*."

"Don't worry because right now this covered pan of rice is going to be ready and with that your body will get back into shape."

"I don't doubt it, brother, but I had a really strange dream and maybe… maybe I should think about packing my suitcases.

"Eat this rice first, slim. And later, let's go to the party at the gringa Evelyn's house tonight. And there you'll escape everything. And with double alum just in case.

"I had forgotten about that party."

"That's what friends are for. To remind you. Take a taste, brother. How is it?"

"It's good. But maybe I should go back to Peru."

"Now I get it. You found the skinny girl who cleans bathrooms and so you want to take off with her."

"She doesn't clean bathrooms. I met her in a bathroom."

"It's great to have sex in the bathroom, isn't it? Although I don't know if it's more hygienic, or dirtier. What do you think, slim?"

"I never had her in the bathroom. I was very young. And when I was fifteen years old the soldiers interrupted me in the middle of going for it."

"The oppression of Latin American dictators has always been screwed up. They don't even let you make out with your little woman."

"That's why everyone ends up screwing here. If you don't believe me, ask Norma and the thousand and one nights. But I can't go without Adriana. I can't weaken now."

"But if you are already skinny, slim."

"Leaving would be to lose the Tank's resurrection, like an abortion without having had fertilization."

"That's a good phrase, brother. I don't understand a damn thing, but it sounds cool. I advise you to make a decision after tonight's blow out."

"Will someone prepare *picante de mondongo* at Evelyn's?"

"I don't know, but I know there will be raw *picante de mondongo*."

And we ended up at the gringa Evelyn's house and upon entering we heard a bullfighter kill at full volume while a flurry of legs pirouetted and backsides following in total rhythm, and Huguito super happy and from the front to the middle of the sea of asses, but I look for a beer to soothe my thirst, *Dos Equis* for the Mexican Revolution and the Institutional Revolutionary Party. And I sit down in a corner. And I separated myself from the party. I separated myself from the bull killing the bullfighter and from the asses and the legs and I thought: two more blood suckings in the lab and maybe I could get my plane ticket to go eat *mondongo*. And Huguito doing the bull killing the bullfighter and I'm toasting health to myself and long live Mexico as long as there is *Dos Equis*, and there, precisely there, in full shout of "Long live Mexico, brother!" a hand on my shoulder, a voice, why aren't you dancing? I turn around, I look, and I continue to look.

"It's because I was waiting for you," I answered her.

"I know. They told me."

Dressed in white coming from out of the sky to the living room of an old Pittsburgh house.

"I know," she repeats again.

The music changes. Her arms surround my neck. My arms surround her life.

"I never dreamed you would come all the way to Pittsburgh."

"I have dreamed many things, but I never dreamed of running into you tonight."

"You look exactly the same, with a few gray hairs, but they look good on you."

"You're the one who looks exactly the same."

"No, not anymore. When did you arrive?"

"For some time now. I lived in Canada and I entered here illegally in a carriage with Amish people."

"Really?"

"Yes."

"You're crazy."

"Who isn't?"

"What were you doing in Canada?"

"I was a political refugee."

"You?"

"So you see the seriousness of the Peruvian crisis, that even political refugees are those of us who don't know shit about politics. And you, where did you get lost that I had to search this entire city?"

"I'll tell you later. I wanted to live alone in the outskirts for a while. Yesterday was the first time I called Marielos for a long time and she told me that you were in Pittsburgh and that surely you would come to this party. I still can't believe it."

"Me neither. Finding you exactly now."

"What's wrong with now?"

"It's because they have granted amnesty and it seems as though I can return to Peru."

"Then you are going to leave soon?"

"I had to find you first."

"Why?"

"Because that's why I have come: to find you and to have a child with you."

"You are definitely crazy."

"Do you want to cure me?"

"And who is going to cure me?"

"What do you think about us curing each other mutually?"

"And if we get even crazier, Tito?"

"It doesn't matter if we have that child and we give him the name I have already thought about."

"You never change."

"Of course I have changed. The first time I saw you, you left me speechless. Now I am speaking to you. That's a tremendous change."

"Let's see your tongue. How many fingers does it measure now?"

"What do you want, Adriana? For me to get an erection while we are dancing?"

"Tito!"

"I'm already getting one anyway."

"I've already realized that also."

"As far as I'm concerned, you could end up pregnant during this song."

Who knows how long Adriana and I were together in my room in Oakland. I told her everything, like I had never done before, how I had promised it to myself when I might see her. I told her about the Tank's death, my dose of guilt for not having rescued him on time, Mañuco's confession, my dream about her to resuscitate Rudy, and all this long pilgrimage to make a dream into reality. She listened to me without making a single commentary and later we went to bed again. And with that answer I thought that she shared the same dream, although she never said anything.

But this time it was around 5:30, the sky was indigo blue, when Adriana got up to pick up her hose, to look for her lost underwear in the middle of the sheets, to put things in order for the day that was coming through the window. She had sat down in a chair and she stretched out one of her legs pulling on her nylon hose when I told her that I was definitely leaving, I'm going to Peru, Adriana. For a second she stopped putting on her hose and her leg stayed frozen in the air.

"I already thought about that, or better yet, I already dreamed it."

"And does it have to be right now?"

The nylon hose started to rise until it covered almost all of her leg. I was leaning on the bed supporting my back on the wall and I had lit a cigarette.

"And what would happen with us if I were to return later?" I told her.

"I don't know."

The other hose began rising up her leg.

"Maybe we would continue seeing each other, right?" she said.

I kept on smoking. I saw her sitting here, half naked and covering her nudity little by little and it seemed to me to be worth crossing the North American border illegally with the fear of being deported, and I looked at her again:

"And if you come to Peru with me, if we forget the United States and we return there together, and if maybe, I don't know, if maybe we have the family that we once dreamed about."

She sat there in silence. She looked for her skirt, her blouse, the sky was still an indigo blue and Adriana finished covering her nudity. She walked toward the window and she smoked, towards the door and she smoked, to the window again and smoking.

"Tito..."

"What, Adriana?"

And a pause, a long pause, almost endless. She was next to the window as if looking towards the river and a childlike speechlessness on my behalf in a Pittsburgh attic.

"Many things have happened."

A growing childlike speechlessness.

"Maybe, maybe one of your friends told you something, but... I," a pause, a lot longer this time, and maybe she swallowed some saliva, "I lost my son shortly after he was born."

I lit another cigarette and I didn't know if I should get close to her and say something to her, who knows what, something that would make her look at me and not at the river of dirty water, but all I did was smoke.

"His name was Fito."

"Adriana…"

"No, please, I've already gone through my period of consolations."

Maybe she held back a tear. I don't know. Maybe one escaped and I didn't realize it. "Not even pills were able to calm me. They even thought about hospitalizing me. Am I surprising you?"

"I didn't know."

"Then the news of Adolfo's scholarship arrived. Going to live in the United States. We would have a Pittsburgh son, can you imagine that? And we laughed, we laughed a lot. And I had some tests run and nothing happened. And later another test, and still nothing happened. I had twenty thousand check ups and twenty thousand treatments, and nothing."

She kept silent for a moment. Not a single noise was heard from outside either. It almost seemed to me that time had frozen still.

"There's not going to be any little Pittsburgh baby in the future," she told me, nor will there be any of another nationality.

"Adriana!"

"Don't tell me that you are very sorry either. I already blamed this city, this country, Adolfo also. I don't know, Tito. I don't know. I might have slept with the first drunk who I saw in a bar only to hurt him? Maybe that's why I moved in with an idiot gringo who only made me laugh? Do you have another cigarette?"

Yes, I had a few. She came close, lit it, she walked around the room always looking towards the window.

"Adolfo also tried to fix things in his own way: closing himself off through his studies in medicine, of course. And forgetting me. He didn't even go to my last appointments. I believe he spent his nights dreaming about his patients' pains. Maybe that might make him happy. And you arrived in the middle of that seaquake. The truth is that I don't know who sent you to call on me, but you made it to Pittsburgh and I couldn't believe

it when Marielos told me that a Peruvian had come from Montreal and that every time he got drunk he said that my tongue
measured three fingers. It couldn't be anyone else, except you.
Then… I don't know, then it was weird, yes, very weird, because I wanted to see you, although I didn't know why. And all
of a sudden, it's like I'm just now realizing it. I'm not sure but
I realize something. You seemed like a new opportunity for me.
Truly, you were like… I don't know… Maybe I also wanted to
return to that bathroom in Mañuco's house when I thought that
you were a mute; or to one afternoon as we were kissing under
the vilca trees and surrounded by a battalion of tanks, do you
remember?, or that day at the front door of my house when we
promised to love each other for the rest of our lives and to have
children at some point and we even talked about names. We had
a good time during those years, didn't we?"

"Yes, we had a good time."

"And with your being here it's as though I believed that we
would be able to relive those years. But…"

"But what, Adriana?"

"It's that I would have liked to run into the old Tito. Really,
that I would have liked. I don't know what for, maybe… maybe
to find the old Adriana?"

"It seems as though we are no longer the same, does it?"

"Yes, that's how it seems. But maybe I wasn't the one who
could take you back to those years in Tacna? To that time when
Rudy was alive and wanted to apply to the university where
you would go. That time where there was you, me, them, when
you and I talked about the name of our first child. Did you ever
think about naming our second son Mañuco? And now you are
telling me that you are going back to Peru and having the family that we always dreamed about… We already know that there
won't be children in our family, that there will never be a first-
born child named Rudy, and that Rudy is dead, assassinated by
Mañuco and neither you nor I can ever bring him back to life
again. Maybe returning to Peru might be the best thing for you,
but for the two of us… I don't know… It's probably because

we are no longer the same as before.

She came close to get another cigarette; she looked me in the eyes.

"You are an important part of my past and I want to keep you like that. And maybe for me it's already time to realize that there will not be a little Pittsburghian, and to tell Adolfo that we need to forgive each other for so many things. If you go to Peru anyway, and if you have a son, don't name him Rudy. It would be better to give him another name. There are so many. And if you see Mañuco, if you see him tell him that I will always remember him and his birthday parties and the bathroom in his house where I once met a boy who I thought was mute. I don't know if you can forgive him. I don't believe that we are able to forgive everything. Nor can we forget either. It's strange, very strange... but never before have I felt so calm, as if all of this time had been a puzzle that I haven't been able to put together until now, as if going back with you to when you were fifteen years old had given me back the peace of my approaching forty years. I hope it is the same for you. Look, dawn has already arrived completely. I didn't realize it, but I think it's going to be a very sunny day. Can I ask you for one thing? I bet you can't guess what. It's that you are so quiet that I would like to know if you have a tongue. Let's see, yes, yes, you have a tongue and it measures three and a half according to Adriana's new scale. And then, why don't you talk? Where is Mrs. Amanda yelling your name throughout the house? Did Mrs. Amanda forget about you this time? Anyway, anyway I have to go. If you go to Peru, and if they ask about me, tell them that I'm okay. You know... maybe this sounds a little exaggerated, but I have never loved you as much as I do now."